THE GOLDEN CHALLENGE

As Civil War looms in England, Belinda tries to escape by fleeing to France with a fortune in gold. But there are others who want her treasure and trying to tell friend from foe makes life both difficult and dangerous. And should she please her father by marrying a man she does not love? For she is increasingly drawn to a man who wants her to abandon everything she knows to face the challenge of life in a new world . . .

SHEILA HOLROYD

THE GOLDEN CHALLENGE

Complete and Unabridged

LINFORD
Leicester

First published in Great Britain in 2010

First Linford Edition
published 2011

British Library CIP Data

Holroyd, Sheila.
  The golden challenge. - -
  (Linford romance library)
  1. Great Britain- -History- -Civil War,
  1642 – 1649- -Fiction. 2. France- -History- -
  Louis XIII, *1610 – 1643*- -Fiction.
  3. English- -France- -Fiction. 4. Love stories.
  5. Large type books.
  I. Title II. Series
  823.9'2–dc22

  ISBN 978–1–44480–603–8

Published by
F. A. Thorpe (Publishing)
Anstey, Leicestershire

Set by Words & Graphics Ltd.
Anstey, Leicestershire
Printed and bound in Great Britain by
T. J. International Ltd., Padstow, Cornwall

This book is printed on acid-free paper

1

His eyes were golden, the long black lashes emphasising their colour. They were also cold and indifferent as he glanced at the girl curtseying before him. Belinda, her silken skirts billowing around her, was annoyed. Men did not ignore her! Daringly, she leaned forward slightly so that if he looked down he would see the curve of her young breasts within the tightly-laced bodice, but when she rose, he was still regarding her with ill-concealed boredom. As the next guest came forward to be introduced Belinda turned away, indignation bringing a flush to her cheeks as she went to share her bad temper with the two girls standing by a window.

'You did not seem to impress Master Hetherington,' Lydia Somers commented with false sympathy.

'Neither has anyone else,' Belinda said crisply. 'At least he might try to hide the fact that no one here interests him and that he cannot wait to get away from us.'

Lydia shrugged. 'The Earl of Ruthington asked Sir Walter to give his brother a bed for the night, and now Sir Walter is parading him round the neighbourhood like a rare animal on display.'

'Well, in this quiet area an Earl's son is a rare animal, I suppose.'

Jane Crompton, the other member of the trio, looked at her companions reproachfully. 'I feel sorry for him. We all know that Master Robert Hetherington has important matters on his mind. His brother wants him to find out how people feel about King Charles' disputes with Parliament. Why should he bother about us?'

'Jane, you are always ready to think of excuses for other people,' Belinda sighed. 'Of course, in this case you are right.'

But the girls did not waste more time discussing Robert Hetherington. Their own affairs were more interesting. They were young and carefree, interested in clothes and trinkets and, above all, in the young men who sought their company. They were in their late teens, ripe for marriage. The status and expectations of the young men of the neighbourhood, and which one would support them and their children for the rest of their lives, occupied a large proportion of their waking thoughts.

Belinda's only problem, it was generally agreed, was in choosing which of her many suitors she liked best. She was, after all, the only child of the wealthy Sir Henry Spence and was generally regarded as something of a beauty, with dark hair and dark eyes often enhanced by a dazzling smile. In private, though, she regretted her firm chin and thought that her nose could have been a little shorter.

Once Belinda had selected a husband, Lydia would be free to choose from the remainder. Her father was comfortably off and she had a blonde, conventional prettiness. Jane might have more difficulty. She was quiet, pleasant-looking but not pretty, and her father had let his estate deteriorate, preferring sporting activities. However, it was thought she would succeed in finding a husband who appreciated a quiet, pious and hard-working wife.

As the buzz of talk continued, Lydia chanced to look round and her eyes widened. Giggling behind her fan, she whispered, 'Stop frowning, Belinda! Here comes Simon!'

Hurriedly Belinda smoothed her skirts and plunged into small talk with Lydia, turning with artificial surprise when someone addressed her.

'Greetings, Mistress Belinda — and to you, Mistress Lydia, and Mistress Jane, of course.'

'Why, Simon!' exclaimed Belinda flirtatiously. 'Has Master Robert been talking to you?'

The young man shook his head. 'He

has been speaking to my father, but my presence was not required. It has given me a chance to see you.'

Simon Gregory was generally regarded as Belinda's probable choice of husband. He was the eldest son of a wealthy baronet and a very personable young man. At barely twenty years old, he was perhaps still a little lanky and gauche, but time would cure that. His morals and behaviour were irreproachable, though Belinda sometimes wondered if she could face a lifetime with someone so serious and lacking in humour. Still, there was no doubt that he was the most eligible bachelor in the neighbourhood. Therefore she regarded him as hers by right, and was annoyed by Lydia's occasional efforts to attract him.

Admitted to the group of young women, Simon was parrying questions about his recent comparative failure in a horse-race when Belinda saw the butler slip unobtrusively through the guests to his master's side and whisper some urgent message. Sir Henry stood still for a few seconds, then clapped his hands together and waited until all faces turned towards him.

'I have just received news,' he announced, 'that His Majesty King Charles recently tried to arrest the five chiefs of the Puritan party in Parliament. But they received prior warning and fled to the city, so that when the king arrived at the Houses of Parliament the birds had flown. Now Charles has abandoned London to Parliament and its supporters.'

There was total silence for a few seconds before Sir Walter Rosford spoke. 'What does this mean for the future?'

Sir Henry regarded his old friend bleakly.

'It means that war is now almost inevitable.'

There was a babble of voices, some blaming Parliament for bringing the country to this state, though others were quietly denouncing Charles as a fool. It might have seemed unthinkable a few years previously that many Englishmen would be prepared to rebel against their king, but by the start of 1642 the prospect of civil war was looming and people who had prayed for peace were having to choose sides, whether they wished to or not.

'If a few hotheads do take up arms,' Belinda overheard one gentleman saying uneasily, 'there is surely no reason why sensible men should not carry on as normal.'

His companion had shaken his head.

'Easier said than done. If the king commandeers your cattle to feed his troops and Parliament takes your corn to feed its army, which side are you going to turn to for help? If you try to remain neutral, you will be seen as an enemy by both.'

'Then of course I shall be loyal to my king.'

The second speaker lowered his voice.

'But will your king be loyal to you? Remember, he allowed his friend

Strafford to go to the scaffold.'

The gathering broke up soon after the dramatic announcement. Men felt the need to go home and consider their options, which side they thought would win, and how they could best preserve their estates and families.

When almost everyone had gone, Sir Henry sought out his daughter.

'Belinda, some gentlemen will be coming here tonight to discuss what this news means, and Master Hetherington has agreed to stay so that he can inform them of his brother's opinions. Will you kindly arrange refreshments for them?'

Dutifully Belinda went in search of the cook and the housekeeper. Her mother had died of a fever five years earlier and Belinda now managed the household very competently. Returning from her errand, she found Robert Hetherington standing alone, staring out of a window at the wintry landscape, giving her the opportunity to observe him. He was tall, his dark hair

8

was cut shorter than was fashionable; he had high cheekbones and a wide, firm mouth. She approached him softly.

'Master Hetherington, do you desire some wine, or is there anything else I can obtain for you?'

He turned with a start, and then shook his head.

'Thank you, but I do not require anything at present, Mistress Belinda.'

So he had at least remembered her name!

His gaze returned to the garden. She hesitated, thinking it impolite to abandon a guest, but wondering whether he would prefer to be left to his thoughts. Before she could decide, he turned to her with a wry smile.

'I beg your pardon. I did not mean to be so abrupt. I was thinking that it is unlikely that hostilities will start in this weather. There should be a couple of months before fighting actually begins.'

She gave an involuntary shiver. For the first time it struck her that a war could affect her own little world. War meant fighting, and people would die.

'This news means that my life, my future, may be very different from what I expected,' she said in a small voice. 'I am afraid that it will affect everyone.'

She remembered something her father had told her.

'I understand you have spent some time in Virginia and planned to go back. Will your plans be altered?'

His face was shadowed. 'Virginia is my home, but now I must see what my brother wishes me to do.'

Before she could say more her father came bustling back.

'Well, I have bid goodbye to everyone. Now we have to wait until evening.' He fidgeted. 'Is there anything you wish to do in the meantime?' His face brightened. 'Would you perhaps like to look at my collection?'

Robert Hetherington looked taken aback. Probably the last thing he had expected that day was to be required to admire some man's hobby. But Sir

Henry's face was eager and expectant.

'My father has a most attractive collection,' Belinda said hastily. 'I am very fond of some pieces myself.'

'What do you collect, Sir Henry?'

'Gold!' was the reply. 'Beautiful things made of gold. Follow me.'

Sir Henry led them up the great staircase to a room linked to his bedchamber by a closet. Here he fumbled with some keys and opened the closet door.

'Wait there and I will bring my best pieces out,' he instructed before disappearing into the closet, soon reappearing with boxes which he held tenderly before opening them to reveal the glitter of gold coins, medallions and items of jewellery.

This collection absorbed much of Sir Henry's time and money, and he was pleased to have a new audience.

'Gold is a marvellous material. Every civilisation has cherished it and made works of art from it,' he declared. 'This medallion was made by Cellini; this coin was discovered in a Roman tomb. This brooch was found in Sussex.' He fingered the brooch lovingly. 'A king may have worn this.'

He picked up another piece. 'Recently I have been fortunate enough to obtain from a Spaniard these pieces from South America.'

To Belinda's relief, Robert Hetherington seemed to appreciate the beauty of the artefacts and the skill of the craftsmen who had made them. However, when he had finished exclaiming over the treasures, he turned to his host with a look of concern.

'There is a king's ransom here. Do many know of your collection?'

'I am proud of it, so I show it to people, but, as you can see, I keep it safely locked away.'

Carefully Robert Hetherington placed a coin back on the table.

'In the future, that may not be enough. Wars are expensive to wage and gold will be in great demand.'

'How will that affect me?' Sir Henry

asked defensively.

'The Parlimentarians could seize your treasure by force. A few locks would not deter them. And if the king asked you to prove your loyalty by giving him your collection to help him finance the war, could you refuse?'

Sir Henry was clutching a handful of coins to him protectively.

'These are the things I love. Surely nobody would take them from me?'

Robert Hetherington's face was grim.

'I fought in the wars in Europe before I went to Virginia. Not only will people seize these beautiful things, they will melt them down for bullion without a second thought. If I were you, Sir Henry, I would try to find some secret hiding place if you do not want these lovely objects destroyed.'

Sir Henry, obviously appalled, was about to protest, but at that moment a servant appeared, announcing the arrival of one of the gentlemen eager to consult Robert Hetherington. Hastily Sir Henry returned his treasures to the closet before leading his guest down-stairs.

Belinda spent a quiet evening by herself, aware of the murmur of voices in the drawing-room, hearing from time to time the sound of horses as men arrived or rode away.

The next morning Robert Hetherington took his leave. He spoke politely to Belinda, but was frowning heavily.

'Did the talks not go well last night?' she enquired.

He sighed impatiently. 'One gentleman's main concern was whether a war would affect his hunting! They do not seem to realise what they face!'

'You must remember that most of them, unlike you, have had no experience of war and cannot yet believe that it will happen here. I myself keep hoping that it is a nightmare from which I will wake.'

'You are right, Mistress Spence. I should have more patience.' A rare smile lit his face. 'I hope that we will meet again so that I can benefit from your wise comments.'

He kissed her hand courteously, and then turned to where Sir Henry stood fidgeting. 'I will take my leave, Sir Henry, and report what we have discussed to my brother.'

★ ★ ★

When Sir Henry and Belinda were alone once more, life seemed to return to normal. The household routine went on, the housekeeper fretted when she found some linen sheets were fraying, and Simon Gregory visited Belinda whenever he could. But there was tension in the air. A maid decided to marry her sweetheart instead of waiting for a summer wedding, 'lest he has to go off fighting.' Sir Henry Spence had made clear his loyalty to the king, but Belinda was aware that he was deeply worried.

One day Simon arrived wearing his best suit of clothes and with a portentous air about him. He found

Belinda in the morning room and she rose and greeted him warmly.

'Simon, I am delighted to see you! It is a cold, depressing day and I would be glad of good company. Have you any news?'

It was the first question people asked each other on meeting nowadays as they waited to hear whether hostilities had begun. Simon sighed.

'There are all kinds of rumours, but no hard news.'

Belinda patted the chair next to her. 'Be seated and talk to me.'

Simon remained standing and shook his head.

'This is not a casual call, Belinda. I have something to ask you.' He cleared his throat and then looked at her, blinking nervously. 'We all know that soon Englishmen will be at war with each other. I have decided that I will ride to serve the king, but when I do that, I would like to leave with the knowledge that the woman I love has promised to marry me. That would comfort me during the turmoil and suffering of a civil war.' He paused and swallowed convulsively. 'Therefore, Belinda, I would like your permission to ask your father for your hand in marriage. Will you marry me?'

Suddenly he was kneeling in front of her, grasping her hand. 'You know well that I love you and I believe that you are fond of me. Please, say you will marry me!'

He kissed the hand he was holding again and again while Belinda stared down at his bent head. She had imagined this scene many times without having finally decided how it would end. Certainly she liked Simon, and he was by far the most eligible bachelor in the neighbourhood — but, inexperienced though she was, she knew that liking was not love.

She was surprised to feel a sudden surge of resentment. Why did he have to force her to decide now? If she accepted him, it would be the end of her girlhood and of her freedom. Then, as she stayed silent, he looked up at her anxiously and her heart melted. It was flattering to be loved so much, and she knew that he would prove to be a good and faithful husband and father. He would do his utmost to give her security in a time of upheaval. What more could she want? She moved her free hand to cover his.

'Yes, Simon. I will marry you.'

There were tears of joy in his eyes as he stood up.

'Then I will go and speak to your father this instant.'

He was gone about thirty minutes — time to find her father in his library, ask for his daughter's hand, receive his consent, say what was fitting — and she spent the time pacing about the room, sure that she had made the right decision, yet wondering why she did not feel happier.

Simon and her father came back together, both smiling broadly. Sir Henry took his daughter's hand and gave it to Simon.

'You have my blessing,' he declared. 'Belinda has been a good daughter to me, but, like any man, I have always wanted a son, and now she will bring me a son-in-law to be proud of.'

Belinda's spirits rose. Of course she had done the right thing!

It was decided that a hurried wedding would not befit the honour and dignity of the two families, and that the marriage would take place when the country's situation was resolved, which it was hoped would not take long.

'We will keep the betrothal informal for the time being,' Sir Henry announced. 'These troubled times are not right for festivities.'

Belinda and Simon agreed, Simon a little more reluctantly.

'Everyone — all our friends — will know that we are promised to each other,' Belinda assured him.

The news spread quickly. Jane Crompton was one of the first to call to congratulate Belinda, and her good wishes were evidently sincere as she hugged her friend.

'You are lucky, Belinda!' she said wistfully. 'You are so pretty, and Simon loves you. I wish I could be as fortunate.'

'You will be,' Belinda assured her warmly. 'You are so kind and helpful and reliable. Once people get to know you, they appreciate that. Just wait until I am married, dear Jane. Then I shall introduce you to dozens of eligible men, and I shall tell them all what a truly wonderful wife you would make.'

Lydia did not consider it worth the effort of a special journey to congratulate Belinda and waited until they met at a mutual friend's. Her congratulations held little warmth.

'At least you are one person who has gained from this awful threat of war, Belinda,' she said acidly. 'It made Master Gregory propose earlier than he intended to do. Otherwise you might have had to wait for a long time.'

Belinda smiled sweetly. 'And has the emergency persuaded anyone to propose to you yet, Lydia?'

Lydia turned away angrily, then lifted her chin. 'Well, now that you no longer have to fend off other admirers, the rest of us are benefiting.'

This was true. Former suitors now saw Belinda as the future property of another man and saved their attentions for unattached young women. Belinda had to admit to herself that she did miss the light-hearted banter and flirtations to which she had become accustomed, but when Simon appeared, proud to be by her side and be seen as her future husband, she smiled up at him, any doubts temporarily forgotten.

2

Some weeks later Sir Henry sought his daughter out. 'My dear, I am afraid I have been neglecting you lately and I know you must be finding life very dull here when the talk is of nothing but war when people do meet. So I have been thinking, and I have decided that it is time you paid to a visit to your Aunt Maria.'

Belinda stared at him, amazed. His sister Maria had married a French count and now divided her time between the court in Paris and their large estates in Normandy. She had shown very little interest in her English niece.

'Has she invited me?'

'Not in so many words,' her father said cautiously. 'I sent her news of your betrothal, of course, and have received a very cordial reply sending you her congratulations. She also mentioned that she and the Comte de Beaumetz have been forced to return to Normandy from the court in Paris because her husband has not been well, though he is recovering. I think this means she would be glad to see you.' He looked at Belinda hopefully. 'After all, my dear, once you are married you will not be free to make such a visit.'

This was true, and the idea of a visit to France had its appeal. But there were obvious difficulties.

'How I would get there? Who would go with me?'

Sir Henry relaxed. Clearly, it was now just a case of deciding the details.

'Well, your maid, Sarah, would have to go with you. I thought John, the groom, could go as well — to look after the horses and act as a bodyguard for the two of you.'

'Could I take our coach to Dover?'

Suddenly Sir Henry was looking decidedly shifty.

'I'm not sure about that. In these

troubled times, it is not wise to draw too much attention to yourself or attract robbers.'

'But I will have little to steal!'

Her father drew a deep breath. Now, evidently, he was coming to the important part.

'Well, I did think — as you are going to France, to my sister — that you could take part of my collection with you and entrust it to her for safe keeping,' he finished in a rush.

So that was it! Her visit to her aunt would merely be a pretext to send his precious gold away from the danger of greedy hands in England!

'No, Father! If anyone knew what I was carrying, I would be a target for every robber in southern England!'

'But no one *will* know. You will merely be a young woman going to visit her aunt, and you will have John to protect you if there is any difficulty.'

Finally, after much persuasion, Belinda agreed to go. She had never crossed the Channel, and it would be a new and exciting experience. However, after some thought, she decided she would prefer to take a companion in case her aunt did not welcome her with open arms — and preferably someone who spoke French, for her own knowledge of the tongue was minimal.

It took some effort, but after Belinda had first tempted Jane with the splendours they would find at her aunt's house, and then had also pointed out that it would be a unique opportunity to improve her knowledge of the French language, Jane Crompton agreed to go with her — after her father was persuaded that he could manage without her for a few weeks.

When Simon heard what was planned, he announced that he could not possibly allow his beloved to travel with only a groom to protect her, and that he also would escort the two gentlewomen and the two servants as far as Dover, where he could help them find a suitable ship to take them across the Channel.

Meanwhile, Sir Henry had to decide which part of his collection he would send to France. Belinda was firm.

'Gold is heavy. I can only take enough to fill a small chest which will fit in a saddlebag.'

Her father protested, and then spent a long time on the heartbreaking task of deciding which of his darlings deserved to be saved, but he finally whittled it down to a manageable quantity. Belinda was uncomfortably aware that the value of what she was taking was still enormous. She would be very relieved to reach her aunt's house safely and pass the responsibility to her. After some discussion, they had agreed not to tell Simon what her luggage would contain. Why worry him with an extra care?

Finally the day came when they set out. Belinda and Jane rode the gentle horses to which they were accustomed, while John the groom had the maid seated behind him and was also leading a pack-horse. Belinda suspected that

Sarah, a giggly and rather foolish girl, had a fondness for John and was most pleased to have an excuse to sit close to the groom with her arms round his waist. Simon was riding his father's best horse with a sword by his side and a pistol thrust into his belt, obviously delighted at the opportunity to appear as a warrior. Sir Henry's parting words had been divided between an affection-ate farewell to his daughter and whispered instructions to take good care of her precious cargo, now carefully padded and packed in a box.

They expected to take two days over the journey to Dover, and planned to spend the night at an inn in Ashford, but after a few hours they realised that the pack-horse was limping badly.

'Will we reach Ashford today?' Simon asked anxiously.

'I'm afraid not, Master Gregory,' answered the groom. 'But don't worry. There's a farm a little way ahead and I know the farmer. He'll help me, and there will be shelter for the ladies while they wait. He and his wife would probably let us stay there the night if we can't sort the matter out quickly.'

After ten minutes' slow progress, they saw a low building set some distance away from the road and they waited on the highway while John dismounted and went to see if help would indeed be available. He disappeared into the house, came out a few minutes later and beckoned to them. No one appeared to greet them, but John nodded at the door.

'The good wife is inside, ma'am, seeing what she can find to give to ladies like yourself.'

They dismounted, leaving the groom to tether the horses, and Simon and Jane led the advance towards the house with Belinda close behind them, eager to find shelter from the cold. Jane was first across the threshold, and Belinda heard an exclamation of surprise, and then a powerful thrust on her own back propelled her forcibly into the house. She almost fell but managed to retain her balance, and turned indignantly to find out what had happened. Then she became aware of her surroundings. There was no welcoming farmer's wife, no warm kitchen fire. Instead the room was dark and cold with a drift of dead leaves on the floor. Nobody had lived here for some time. Bewildered, she looked back at the door where John stood and saw, in disbelief, that he was holding a pistol.

'What are you doing with that? Put it away! And where are the farm folk?'

He did not move or reply, merely grinned wolfishly at her. She felt a tingle of fear. Glancing round, she saw Simon and Jane looking equally at a loss. Then Belinda saw Sarah peering over John's shoulder.

'Sarah! Tell this man to stop being so stupid!'

But at her words, Sarah gathered up her skirts and turned and fled.

'She won't be coming back to help you,' John said roughly. 'My brother will be here within the hour and she is going back up the road a short way to guide him to us.'

Now Simon strode forward, doing his best to appear authoritative and commanding. 'What game are you playing?'

John's grin grew wider and he nodded at Belinda.

'You mean your sweetheart hasn't told you? Didn't she trust you?'

Simon looked at Belinda enquiringly and she bit her lip.

'She still doesn't want to tell you?' John jeered. 'Then let me. You've got a saddlebag full of gold on one of those horses.'

'There can't be. Mistress Spence would have told me!'

Belinda's head was lowered. 'It was simply that my father and I didn't wish to worry you, Simon.'

John was laughing. 'But I knew! The servants saw Sir Henry sorting out the best coins and wrapping them. When I think of all the time my brother and I have spent trying to think of some way of getting at the gold in that closet without being caught! And then your father asked me to take care of you — *and* the gold!'

'If you steal it from us, you will soon be caught! I'll get the nearest magistrate to raise such a hue and cry that you won't be able to hide anywhere in England!' Simon said vehemently.

John was laughing again. 'My brother always said you were stupid, gentleman or not. Do you think we are going to leave you alive to bear witness against us?'

Belinda felt cold horror and Jane screamed. Simon tugged desperately at the pistol in his belt, fumbled with it inexpertly, and then dropped it. He scrambled to pick it up but tripped on a loose flagstone and fell just as John fired. The shot passed harmlessly over Simon's head and buried itself in the far wall, but there was a cry of pain from Simon on the floor and he sat up clutching his leg.

'The clumsy idiot has twisted his

ankle,' John said, contemptuously kicking aside the pistol Simon had let fall.

Jane dropped to her knees beside Simon while Belinda swung round to face John.

'You cannot get away! Everybody knows you set out with us.'

'And that is all they will know! It will be weeks before anyone wonders what has happened to you because everyone will think you are in France.' He nodded at Simon, who was groaning as Jane inspected his ankle. 'This just makes things easier for us.' His expression became a leer. 'Maybe my brother and I will be able to enjoy ourselves with you two young ladies before we dispose of you.'

He stepped nearer to Belinda, stretching out a hand to touch her. Fury rose and overcame her fear. Striking his arm aside, she then kicked him hard on the knee. He stumbled, and with her other arm she hit him with such force that he fell, striking his head on a corner of the stone fireplace.

There was an unpleasant sound like a stone hitting a wall, and he did not move.

Absolute silence reigned for a few seconds.

'You've killed him!' breathed Jane in horror.

'Good!' Belinda replied, kicking John's prone body viciously. There was no movement, no response. Satisfied, Belinda turned her back on him and knelt beside Simon.

'Where have you hurt yourself? Is it bad?'

He could only groan as she touched his ankle.

'He needs a surgeon,' Jane declared, but Belinda shook her head.

'How are we going to get a surgeon? It would mean one of us going off alone to find one, and we don't know which way to go.'

'But he is badly hurt!'

'Nonsense!' Belinda said firmly, trying to convince herself as much as Jane. 'It's really only a sprained ankle.'

'I'll be all right soon,' Simon told them. He tried to stand but could not bear any weight on his ankle and sank down again.

Jane swayed and Belinda looked at her fiercely.

'Jane! If you swoon now, I shall never forgive you! I need your help.'

With a visible effort Jane stayed upright, her gaze fixed on Simon's face, while with teeth gritted Belinda removed his boot and drew down his stocking. Simon clenched his fists in evident agony and she could see that his ankle was swelling.

'Jane, we need something to bind it! Tear a piece off your petticoat.'

White-faced, Jane did as she was bid, tearing off enough strips so that the ankle could be padded and roughly bound while Simon sat with his eyes shut and teeth gritted. Then, as the two girls stared at him, he looked up at them with a shaky smile. Belinda gave a sigh of relief and managed to smile down at him in return.

'You will be all right soon,' she assured him, but now he was staring at John's body.

'He can't harm us,' Belinda told him, but he shook his head.

'*He* can't,' he whispered, 'but he said his brother would be here soon.'

His brother and the girl Sarah, and possibly other accomplices! Belinda stood up hastily.

'We can't let ourselves be found here. We would be trapped.'

'We must return to your father's,' Jane told her. Belinda regretfully dismissed this idea.

'If we retrace our steps, we might walk right into them.'

She put her hands on her hips and thought for a moment.

'Simon, if we can get you to a horse, do you think you could stay on until we reach Ashford? Then we can find a magistrate, report what has happened, and send a message to my father.'

As he nodded, she saw that now Jane's gaze of fascinated horror was fixed on John's body.

'I'll drag that outside and hide it. Can you help me, Jane?'

Jane gulped and turned even paler, and made no effort to move. Belinda glared at her impatiently. 'Very well, stay where you are. I will see to it.'

It took all her strength to drag the groom's body out of the cottage and conceal it under some bushes. It did occur to her that perhaps she should feel whether John's heart was beating or whether he was indeed dead, but she could not bring herself to touch his bare flesh. Breathless, she went to inspect the horses, which were still tethered where John had left them when he lured them into the farm-house. She went back into the cottage and slowly, as Simon tried valiantly to conceal his pain, the two girls helped him stand and managed to get him outside and into the saddle of his own horse. The saddlebags were transferred to the girls' horses and the other two horses were turned loose, a lucky find for whoever came across them. At the last minute, her foot on the stirrup, Belinda hesitated.

'John might have a knife or some other weapon that we could use. I'll just look and see.'

But the body of the groom was gone. Only the crushed vegetation showed where it had lain. He must have recovered his senses after all! She shivered. Was he in the nearby bushes now, watching for a chance to spring on her? She picked up her skirts and ran back to where the other two were waiting for her.

'Let us hurry,' she commanded, mounting her horse as quickly as she could. 'Time is passing and John's brother may be here at any moment.'

She set a fast pace, desperate to get away from the farm, ignoring Jane's protests that the speed was jarring Simon and causing him unnecessary suffering. Belinda was well aware how painful the ride was for him, how he was lying along his horse's neck, just managing to hold on, but there was nothing she could do.

'A little pain doesn't matter now,' Belinda told Jane. 'The sooner we can get him to Ashford and a doctor, the sooner he can get proper attention. It is growing late and the light is beginning to fail already. Do you want to be still on the road when it is dark, with John's brother on our trail?'

Thankfully, this put an end to the protests and soon Belinda was calculating that it could not be more than half an hour to Ashford. Then someone with authority would take care of Simon, find food and shelter for herself and Jane, and send a message to her father.

Even as her heart was lifting at this thought, the little cavalcade rounded a corner and saw that the road was blocked by a fallen tree. A tall, fleshy man stood in front of it, barring their way. There was a pistol in his hand.

Belinda pulled her horse to a rough halt, but before either she or her companions could turn and flee, another man had stepped into the road behind them, cutting off their retreat. It was John, the groom, with his head roughly bandaged.

'We've got them now, Tom!' he shouted triumphantly. 'And I am going to make her pay for what she did to me!'

'Silence!' snarled his brother. 'We're not wasting any time. We'll kill them and take the gold. That will be revenge enough.'

The pistol in his right hand was pointed at Belinda and she heard the click as he cocked it. Automatically she shut her eyes and tensed herself to receive the shot. Then there was the sound of galloping hooves behind them and a horseman burst into sight, riding John down before he could move.

Tom roared with fury, but the rider was on him before he could bring his pistol to bear and the tip of a riding boot caught him under the chin and sent him reeling to the ground, his firearm lost. The ambushers started to scramble to their feet, then froze as a second horseman appeared, a pistol at the ready in each hand.

Robert Hetherington, the first rider, dismounted and picked up Tom's pistol. Then he strode up to John and checked him for weapons, taking a knife from his belt. Only then did he turn to Belinda.

'You are safe now,' he said.

3

As they gazed at their rescuers in amazement, Robert Hetherington's manservant menaced the two would-be robbers with his pistol and his master went across to Simon Gregory. Simon, pale-lipped and with his hair damp with sweat, struggled to thank him, but their rescuer shook his head.

'Never mind politeness. I was told you'd been hurt. What happened?'

'He tripped over his feet and succeeded in spraining his ankle,' Belinda informed him tartly.

The golden eyes swept over her coldly but otherwise Robert ignored her.

'You have done well to get so far, lad. Do you think you can carry on just a bit further?'

Simon nodded dumbly, and Robert turned to the two girls.

'It is a ten-minute ride to Ashford, and then your ordeal will be over.'

Belinda gestured at John and his brother, both groaning and with hands clasped to their heads but not daring to move as the servant's pistols were aimed steadily at them. 'What about these?'

Robert surveyed them with contempt.

'Bind their hands and feet,' he ordered his servant. 'I'll get that wench.'

He disappeared back the way they had come and shortly reappeared virtually dragging along a young woman — Sarah, Belinda's maid. Her wrists were tied and she was gagged, but the venomous looks she cast at her mistress spoke volumes.

Robert Hetherington and his servant trussed up John and his brother roughly, in spite of their screams of pain, and dumped them like sacks across one of the horses. Robert mounted his own horse.

'Follow us, and take the men and the girl to the magistrate in Ashford,' he told his servant. 'Tell him what has happened, and that I will call on him tomorrow to give him the details. Then come to the Swan Inn.'

The man nodded, and Robert gestured to the other riders to follow him. Looking back, Belinda saw the man plodding along leading with one hand the horse with the two men loaded on it, his other hand gripping Sarah's arm and forcing the unwilling girl onwards.

'Can he manage all three of them by himself?' she asked anxiously.

'Two wounded men and a girl? That will be no problem for Harry.'

Belinda and Robert Hetherington took the lead, with Jane and Simon lagging behind a little.

After expecting to be shot dead and then suddenly rescued, Belinda was in a state of shock, but after a while she recovered enough to look at Robert Hetherington and see how tightly his lips were pressed together.

'You look angry,' she ventured, and was taken aback when he turned to her in fury.

'Of course I am angry! Didn't your father realise what a temptation his gold would be to a servant? Had he no more sense than to send you off with only that hopeless young idiot to guard you?'

The colour rose in Belinda's cheeks. 'Simon and I are betrothed. Of course he wished to come with me, to protect his future wife.'

Robert Hetherington stared. 'You are betrothed? To Simon Gregory?'

She nodded. Hetherington looked at Simon, then back at Belinda, and fell silent, leaving her guiltily aware that she herself had no high opinion of Simon as a protector.

It was a relief when Ashford finally appeared before them.

'My father has reserved rooms for us at The Swan,' Belinda informed Hetherington.

'I know,' he replied curtly.

Finally they rode through the arch

into the coaching yard of The Swan Inn and were able to hand over their tired horses to the care of the ostlers. Robert helped Simon indoors and ordered the innkeeper to send for a surgeon immediately before taking the young man upstairs. Meanwhile Belinda took good care that their baggage, including the saddlebag containing the gold, was never out of her sight until it was safely in the chamber reserved for her and Jane. The innkeeper's wife promised Belinda and Jane hot water to wash themselves, as well as food and drink.

'Thank you. As quickly as possible, please,' Belinda responded, ushering the woman out of the room. Then she threw herself on the bed.

'What a day! This was supposed to be a quiet ride through the country. Instead we have narrowly escaped death — twice!'

Jane had sunk into a chair. 'It has been terrible! And poor Simon is hurt.'

'It was his own fault — he shouldn't have been so clumsy. But now all seems to be turning out for the best,' Belinda said cheerfully — and then recoiled in shock as Jane turned on her, face flaming and with tears of fury in her eyes.

'You mean it's turning out well for *you*! Did it ever occur to you and your father that your little scheme to smuggle his gold abroad put Simon and me in danger as well as yourself, without you even having the grace to ask us if we were willing to take that risk? Now poor Simon has been hurt and it is only through good fortune that we were not both raped and killed! To make matters worse, you are supposed to love Simon; you are going to be his wife, yet instead of caring for him you speak about him as if he were a clumsy fool, a nuisance!'

Furious, Belinda opened her mouth to defend herself but found she had nothing to say. Jane was quite right. She swallowed, and thought hard.

'I apologise, Jane. You are right as far

as keeping you ignorant of the gold is concerned, but we trusted John. He had served us for a long time. As for Simon, I do care, but my head was in a whirl of shock and I reacted badly. I know it was wrong, and I will try and make it up to him. But it does look as though we are safe now.'

Jane was still endeavouring to hold back her tears, and Belinda held out her arms. 'Please forgive me.'

Her friend hesitated, and then ran into her friend's embrace.

'I was so frightened!' she wailed.

'And so was I, and I won't keep any more secrets from you. Now, is there anything else worrying you?'

Jane sniffed and nodded. 'Do you think people will be shocked by two young unmarried women travelling the country with two unmarried men?'

Belinda had to check a laugh. 'Oh, people are concerned with greater worries at the moment — and not many will question the behaviour of the younger brother of an earl.'

This seemed to calm Jane's fears of impropriety.

The inkeeper's wife was soon back with a tray of refreshments, accompanied by a maid with jugs of hot water, together with the news that the surgeon was already examining Simon. Twenty minutes later, Robert knocked on their door.

'How is Simon?' Belinda asked him.

He allowed himself a small smile. 'You may come and see for yourself.'

It was a relief to see that Simon was now resting comfortably in bed. On seeing them he even managed a weak smile.

'The surgeon said it is a bad sprain, but that is all, and it should heal without trouble,' he said. His eyes lingered on Belinda. 'I am sorry I was so clumsy. I was supposed to protect you, and instead I became a burden.'

Safe, clean and fed, Belinda had had time to forgive his clumsiness and patted his hand affectionately.

'Accidents happen. You were taken by

surprise. You didn't know there was any reason for John to turn against us.'

'Is it really true about the gold?' His lips twisted when Belinda nodded and he turned his face away. 'I wish you had felt able to confide in me.'

'It was my father's decision,' Belinda excused herself, uncomfortably aware that she had been in full agreement.

'Now let the lad get some rest,' Robert interrupted. 'Our dinner will be ready in ten minutes. I shall meet you downstairs.'

Belinda turned to go, and it was Jane who lingered.

'Are you truly all right?' Belinda heard her murmur anxiously, and saw Simon smile at her reassuringly.

Belinda went down for dinner with a good appetite, but once Jane had swallowed her soup she pushed her chair back and stood up shakily.

'I am sorry, but I cannot eat any more. I am too tired.'

Once she had gone, Robert and Belinda ate in silence, until Belinda, spooning up the last of her apple pie, turned to him to demand answers.

'How did you know where we were, and that we were in danger?'

He sat back, sipping a glass of wine.

'I had a message for your father from my brother, the earl, and when I asked permission to pay my respects to you I was told that you were on your way to France to visit your aunt. After what I had seen at your house before, I suspected that this sudden decision to go to France might have something to do with preserving your father's treasure. A little questioning, a little pressure, and your father confirmed my guess.' His mouth twisted. 'As I said, I could not believe that he had been foolish enough to send two girls and a maidservant off with a groom and a load of gold and with only a young lad to look after you. In any case I had to come this way, so I followed your route, and Harry and I found your maid Sarah in an alehouse.

'She panicked when I asked her

where you were, and why she was not with you, and tried to slip out of the back of the house, but I had Harry waiting there. After that, in between protesting how she had been forced to help the pair of rascals, she told me the whole story — how she had been waiting for the groom's brother when suddenly John appeared, scarcely able to walk, and told her he had been knocked unconscious and that the three of you had escaped. His brother came along soon afterwards and she heard the two of them decide to cut across country and set up the ambush on the Ashford road, so we came in search of you. We'd been following you for some time when you rode into the ambush.'

'But we didn't hear you — you just suddenly appeared.'

Robert grinned.

'My dear Mistress Spence, Harry and I are experienced hunters. We have tracked wild animals in the Americas where our lives depended on our skill and silence. Following you was child's play once we made sure that the girl could not warn the rascals.'

'So what happens next?' Belinda asked.

'What happens next is that you follow your friend upstairs and go to bed,' Robert Hetherington told her with calm authority. 'We will decide what to do about this sorry mess tomorrow.'

He stood, Belinda following his lead. She was about to wish him goodnight when suddenly she was seized by an uncontrollable fit of trembling and had to grasp the back of her chair to keep upright. Robert was by her side in a second, supporting her with an arm round her waist.

'I don't know what is the matter with me,' she managed to murmur.

'You are finally reacting to the fact that you have been facing violent death,' he told her. 'I am surprised you haven't collapsed completely. You must be tougher than you look. How do you feel now?'

'Better,' she told him, then looked up at him anxiously. 'You will look after us, won't you?'

He nodded. 'Of course I will. Now go to bed. Goodnight.'

'Goodnight,' she replied, and lifted her face to him as trustingly as a child. He hesitated, then kissed her gently on the forehead.

'Master Gregory is a very lucky man,' he said softly.

★   ★   ★

It took a great effort for Belinda to climb the stairs and undress herself, missing her maid's usual assistance. She fell into the great bed next to Jane and was instantly asleep, only waking the next morning when her friend stirred as the maid brought in water for their toilet. She sat up, looked around at the unfamiliar surroundings and then remembered the previous day. She threw back the covers.

'Wake up, Jane! We have to decide

what to do next.'

Jane clutched the bedclothes to her. 'Belinda, all I want is to go home!'

Belinda looked at her reproachfully. 'There's no need to be frightened. Master Hetherington and his man are looking after us.' She stopped suddenly. 'I suppose I must see if Simon is any better.'

'I looked in when I came to bed and he was sleeping soundly then,' volunteered Jane, instantly making Belinda feel guilty because it had not occurred to her to do the same. However, there was no reason for worry. Simon had had breakfast and had even been shaved by the manservant, Harry. He was still pale, with dark shadows under his eyes, but stoutly refused to regard himself as an invalid.

'I shall be up and dressed soon,' he informed Belinda. 'Master Hetherington has gone to see the magistrate, and when he returns he and I will decide what we should do next.'

Belinda looked at him coldly.

'After you have consulted Jane and myself, I suppose?'

'Of course we will take your wishes into account,' he said hastily.

Belinda went off to breakfast, fuming at the easy masculine assumption of superiority.

Robert came back to the inn soon afterwards with the news that the magistrate had been informed of everything that had happened the previous day, and that the maid had repeated her story, so the two brothers were now securely imprisoned and would stay there until they could be tried.

'And now we have to decide what to do,' he said grimly.

'Surely that is obvious!' cried Jane. 'We must go back, so that Simon can be cared for until his ankle is better.'

Simon flushed. 'I have recovered, Jane. There is no need to make any more fuss over me.'

Robert turned to Belinda. 'What do you advise?'

She had been thinking about this

since she woke up.

'What Jane advises — going home — is the obvious course of action,' she said slowly. 'However, that means I will not see my aunt and I will not have saved my father's treasure. If I return, he will only try to devise some other way of getting it to her.'

'Then Simon and I can return, and you can go on!' Jane exclaimed, but Belinda shook her head.

'It is obviously impossible for me to go to France without an escort to protect me and the treasure.'

'Then I will got to France with you!' declared Simon. 'Jane, you don't really want to miss your visit to France, do you?'

Jane's expression indicated the opposite, but she said nothing and there was a thoughtful silence, broken by Robert Hetherington.

'So Simon and Belinda are for going on to France, and Jane is undecided. Simon, I admire your courage, but you are still suffering and it might still be difficult for you to travel.

'However, I had myself intended to go to France in the near future, so may I propose that I come with the three of you? I have a few days to spare. The two ladies can visit the countess as was planned. Simon, you can come along with us instead of attempting to travel home on your own. With Harry, that means there will be three men accompanying and guarding two ladies.'

Belinda's eyes sparkled. The adventure could continue! Simon nodded, hardly concealing his relief that he would not, after all, be the sole protector of Belinda and Jane, and even Jane looked as if this offer eased her worries.

'What do you say?' Robert asked, then looked at their faces and laughed. 'I think I can take it that you accept my offer. Very well, I shall ride ahead to Dover and find a ship which will take us across the Channel. The rest of you can follow more slowly.'

Belinda and Jane went up to their room to pack.

Robert had already left when they came downstairs but Simon was waiting for them and taking his responsibilities very seriously, checking the horses and the luggage, asking the ladies if there was anything else they needed for the journey. He had already arranged for a message to be sent to his father explaining his delay in returning home. Meanwhile Harry quietly and efficiently saw that everything was in order, and they were soon on horseback and riding out of Ashford.

As they rode, Belinda was reviewing her recent behaviour in the light of Jane's accusations the previous day. She had to acknowledge that she had been at fault. Trying to make amends, she moved closer to Simon, knowing that Jane would note how attentive Belinda was being to her future husband. She was therefore disappointed when Simon showed no appreciation of her behaviour, only responding briefly to what she said or merely nodding curtly. Then she noticed how his lips were pressed tightly together and how tense he looked, and she realised that he was still in pain but trying to conceal it from everyone. Like the others, she fell silent.

The hours passed slowly. At midday they ate a light meal at an inn before continuing on their way. The sun was beginning its decline when the little party reached a high point dividing two gentle valleys and Belinda, looking at the horizon, saw that beyond the rolling hills and woodland of southern England there was a straight line dividing the sky from a grey, flat expanse.

'The sea!' Belinda breathed. 'Look — it is the sea!'

It was the first time she had ever seen the coast and she stared hungrily. Beyond that stretch of water was France. All that she was familiar with — the customs, the habits, even the language — would be left behind her when she crossed the sea.

Now the end of their journey was in

sight they quickened their pace, entering Dover as night began to fall. They were not used to cities where the streets were full and noisy after dark, and were relieved to reach the inn where they had arranged to lodge overnight. Robert Hetherington was already there, ready to welcome them with his news, and Belinda's spirits lifted at the sight of his tall figure.

'I have found a ship,' he announced.

At the supper table he gave them more details.

'We sail in the morning. Our horses will be stabled at this inn until we return. We can hire or buy horses in Calais.' He frowned at them. 'You do not seem very interested in these arrangements.'

'Frankly, Master Hetherington, I think the three of us are more worried about the sea crossing at this moment,' Belinda confessed.

None of them had ever set foot on a ship, and their way to the inn had taken them past the craft anchored in the harbour. They had seen through the masts to the sea covered with white-tipped waves, and suddenly the Channel had seemed a more formidable obstacle than they had imagined.

Robert Hetherington laughed. 'Just over a score of miles? A few hours at sea? That is nothing. Remember, Harry and I have spent weeks at sea on our voyages to and from Virginia, and we survived some rough passages.'

'Was it worth it?' Simon ventured.

Robert's gaze became abstracted, as though he was looking at something a long way away.

'I admit we sometimes doubted that when we were being driven along by a storm, but when we got there all our sufferings were forgotten.'

'Is Virginia so beautiful?'

'Yes,' Robert answered emphatically. 'Virginia is beautiful. It is fertile and welcoming, but we did not endure weeks at sea just for that. Beyond Virginia there is a vast, unknown land. I have travelled there and seen birds and

61

animals that no one in England has ever seen, and no matter how far I have gone I know that there is still far more waiting to be discovered.'

He looked at their politely puzzled faces and grinned.

'Anyway, believe me when I tell you that a few hours at sea are endurable. The boat we are going on is not luxurious, but it will get us there safely. Now, we have to be up at dawn, so I suggest we retire to bed.'

4

Belinda was bone-weary after two days on horseback, and the maid's knock on the door had to be repeated before she roused herself. It might be dawn, but the sky was still dark, covered with heavy clouds. The party shivered in driving rain as they made their way to the docks, where they stared in surprise at the ship Robert Hetherington indicated.

'But it is so small!' was Belinda's reaction.

'All you need is a cabin where you can sit for a few hours.'

'Ugh!' she complained, covering her face in disgust. 'It stinks of fish!'

'Naturally it does. It is a fishing vessel,' he said impatiently.

'Was there not anything better available for the ladies?' Simon asked. Robert turned on him.

'Yes, there are large, comfortable vessels, but their passengers are liable to be under surveillance by the king's men and parliamentarian spies. You are trying to smuggle a fortune in gold out of the country at a time when the king and his enemies both need all the money they can get. You do not want to draw attention to yourselves! The captain of this ship, The Pelican, catches fish, but he also carries people who wish to leave the country unobtrusively. Do you think that you can find more suitable transport?'

There was no reply to that, and they carefully negotiated the gangplank to be welcomed by a man who said he was the captain but was as unshaven and unkempt as the rest of the crew. As soon as they were aboard, the crew began to prepare for departure.

The captain offered to show them to a cabin which they were welcome to occupy during the crossing, but the smell of fish grew even stronger when they started to go below and they unanimously decided to stay on deck. Harry was soon mingling with the crew, the others watching as the ship set sail for France and gradually Dover was left behind. However, once the shelter of the harbour was gone, the ship felt the force of the wind-driven waves, and first Jane and then Simon decided that they needed to go below after all. Belinda stayed where she was, untroubled by the lurching deck, watching the sailors deftly controlling the ropes and sails.

'They are so quick, and they never seem to get in each other's way,' she marvelled to Robert.

He nodded briefly but said nothing and, when she made some other comment, instead of acknowledging it he turned away abruptly and hurried to the stern of the boat.

'It looks as though you are the only one of your party who isn't troubled by seasickness, mistress,' said the captain dryly.

Belinda shook her head.

'Master Hetherington can't be sick.

He has been to Virginia and back several times. He couldn't have endured that if he was ill all the time.'

The captain looked at Robert, who was now leaning over the rail, with renewed interest. 'He's been to the Americas, has he? Well, a lot of men are seasick for the first few days but then recover. Indeed I was like that myself, the first few voyages I made.'

'Have you been to the Indies, or Virginia?'

The captain nodded. 'Twice, when I was younger.'

'Did you like it there? Would you have liked to stay?'

He took his time before replying. 'I liked it a great deal. I felt it was a new country where I would have a chance to make a new life for myself. But I didn't stay. I had a sweetheart and my parents waiting for me in England, so I had to choose, and I chose England.' He sighed. 'I've regretted it sometimes. In England, too much depends on who your father was. There, once you reached the forests and the wilderness, you felt you would be judged on what you alone did for yourself, not what your family had done.'

Barking orders at his crew, he left them. Robert Hetherington still clung to the rail, so Belinda made her way below decks to see how the other two were faring. Although not actively ill, they were lying on the rough bunks fitted in the cabin, eyes fast shut, shuddering faintly when a larger wave than usual struck the boat. Belinda managed to persuade one of the crew to fetch her a basin of water and bathed their foreheads gently, and Jane seemed to find that her little bottle of smelling salts containing spirit of hartshorn eased her suffering.

The ship began to sail more smoothly as if the waves were lessening, and eventually Belinda settled in a decrepit armchair and fell into a doze. She woke abruptly to find that the ship seemed to have stopped moving. Had they reached France?

On deck she saw Robert Hetherington and the captain conferring by the light of a lantern.

'Why have we stopped?' she asked anxiously.

'The wind has failed, and now we are stuck here at the mercy of any king's ship that sees us,' Robert answered impatiently. He turned back to the captain. 'How much longer to Calais, now we have lost the wind?'

The captain licked his finger and held it up.

'There's a breeze starting,' he said comfortably. 'Then we will be in Calais in little more than an hour, and you can be about your business, whatever that is.'

Robert gave a harsh sigh of relief.

'At least you seem to feel better,' Belinda remarked tartly and he looked at her with disfavour.

'May I suggest that you go below once more and prepare your friends for our landing?'

The captain's forecast proved to be correct. Calais seemed as familiar to him as Dover, and there were several shouts of welcome as his vessel nosed into a berth. The party of passengers found an inn and then breakfasted while Harry negotiated the hire of suitable horses, and soon after noon they were on their way again.

* * *

They allowed three days for the journey to Beaumetz, and Belinda found most of it rather dull. True, everyone they encountered spoke a different language, but Robert dealt with that problem, as he seemed to do with all others. The scenery was not markedly different to that of her homeland, and the inns were adequate but not outstanding.

Simon had recovered rapidly and now suffered little discomfort. Jane was a timid rider, as well as obviously a little in awe of Robert Hetherington, and Simon, still nursing his ankle, tended to ride with her, leaving Belinda to ride ahead with Robert. Belinda enjoyed his company. He spoke to her as an equal, talking of his travels and adventures, teaching her something of the world that lay beyond the confines of her quiet life with her father.

'Does our journey spoil your plans?' she asked him at one time.

He shook his head. 'You have given me an excuse to come to France which disguises my real purpose — to find out the reactions of certain Frenchmen to the prospect of civil war in England.'

They rode in silence for a while and then she said hesitantly, 'If there is war, will you fight for the king or go back to Virginia?'

'I shall be obliged to stay and fight,' he said heavily. 'Charles is my king.'

'But from what you have said from time to time, you do not have a high opinion of him.'

'Indeed I have not! The man is a fool. He talks about 'the divine right of kings' but seems to forget that a king has a duty to his subjects. He has made some exceedingly stupid decisions.'

'Yet you are still prepared to fight for him?'

70

'As I said, he is my king. It is a question of duty.' He thought for a while. 'In a way, I can understand Charles. His elder brother, Prince Henry, was a very promising heir to the throne. Then Henry died and Charles, instead of being the unimportant second son, found that he was to become king. Suddenly he had power.'

Belinda's eyes were on his face.

'Is that how you see yourself, as the 'unimportant second son'?'

His mouth twisted wryly. 'I sometimes forget, Mistress Belinda, that you are very intelligent. Yes, I have known what it is to be the second son who is surplus to requirements, for whom there is no clear role. The younger sons of noblemen usually settle for the army or the church. I tried soldiering but did not find it agreeable. Nor am I suited to the Church. There was a time when I wondered what to do with my life, but my brother is a very perceptive man. He sent me to Virginia to check on how his estates there were being run, and there

71

I found a life I could enjoy; a purpose.'

'The captain of the Pelican mentioned that one's birth does not matter so much in the Americas.'

'There is still snobbery among the owners of the tobacco plantations, but you are free of that once you reach the lands where your survival depends on your ability and not on your family. In any case, it is not a problem for you to worry about. You are a young woman of respectable birth and you are going to marry a young man of the same class.'

Belinda gave him a scornful glance. 'You have forgotten something, Master Hetherington. I am a woman — therefore every man, regardless of his birth or intelligence, regards me as an inferior. There is nowhere I can go which will change that!'

Robert looked startled. 'I apologise. I had never thought of that.' He smiled. 'I promise I will try to regard women as equal to men unless proved otherwise. Meanwhile, as we are growing so intimate, do call me Robert.'

As Beaumetz drew nearer, Belinda's companions sought more information about their future hosts and she told them what she knew.

'My Aunt Maria married the Count of Beaumetz about fifteen years ago and has not returned to England since, so I hardly remember her. She met him in London when she was at the Court, and he was with the French Ambassador. My aunt is his second wife and he is several years older than she. They have no children. That is all I know.'

'Is your aunt expecting you?' Simon said anxiously, fearful of offending social codes by appearing at the Count's gates as an uninvited guest.

'My father informed me he was going to send her a message,' was all Belinda could say to reassure him.

Although unsure of their welcome, the little party was looking forward to the end of the journey. However Aunt Maria felt about them, she could not refuse hospitality to her niece or those who had helped her.

They expected the Count's residence to at least equal the manor-houses they had known in England, but when a Frenchman was persuaded to guide them to their destination, the reality stunned them. He led them to a great castle set amid carefully tended parkland. The building was obviously centuries old, but some large windows indicated that it had been adapted to suit modern tastes. They gazed at it in awe.

'This is . . . most impressive,' Simon said with considerable restraint.

'Even my brother might envy this,' commented Robert.

Belinda swallowed. 'It is not quite what I was expecting,' she said coolly, 'but I look forward to enjoying my aunt's hospitality here.' She urged her horse on towards the approach to the entrance. Their arrival was noted by gardeners and other servants, and when they reached the great door it was opened almost before Harry could knock to announce their presence. After a short discussion, he returned to the waiting party.

'The Countess does not seem to be expecting us,' was his bad news. 'However, we have been invited to enter the castle while she is informed of our arrival.'

The room into which they were ushered might only be an antechamber, but it was furnished with luxury that displayed considerable wealth. Belinda eyed the impressive fittings, the velvet and silk upholstery and curtains, and mentally compared the sumptuous style to the comfortable but slightly worn surroundings of her own home.

Soon the door was opened by a footman and a lady swept in. She was aged about thirty-five, and dressed in an elaborate gown that seemed more suited to a royal court than a stay in the country. She was also frowning, evidently at the unexpected arrival of so many would-be guests.

Belinda and Jane curtsied deeply, while Simon and Robert swept elaborate bows.

'I am informed that one of you claims to be my niece,' the lady began, a little haughtily, and then stopped, staring at Belinda. Suddenly she smiled broadly and clapped her hands. 'Ah, that must be you! You look just like your poor mother!'

Belinda smiled. 'And I was just thinking how you resemble my father!'

The Countess threw back her head and laughed.

'That is not quite so flattering, but I am afraid it is true! But what are you doing here? And who are your companions?'

'My father was supposed to have sent you a message to explain everything, ma'am, but clearly you have not yet received it. I am here on an errand for him.' She gestured at the others. 'May I present my friend and companion, Miss Jane Crompton? This gentleman is my betrothed, Master Simon Gregory. He did not intend to come to France — but that is a long story which I must tell you later.' She turned to Robert.

'Finally, may I present the man who saved our lives — Master Robert Hetherington, brother of the Earl of Ruthington.'

This last morsel of information evidently erased any remaining doubts that Aunt Maria might have been feeling. 'Then you are all very welcome.'

The Countess led them into the inner rooms of the castle. Here more wealth was displayed in artistic treasures such as tapestries and bronzes and finely inlaid furniture. She urged them to be seated, and sent servants for refreshments. Apparently the Count was in his study, but a servant hurried off to tell him of the new arrivals.

He soon appeared, a man of about sixty, limping a little from the gout which afflicted him and which had forced his withdrawal from the Court. He was very dignified, and courteous rather than welcoming to his unexpected guests. After the ritual of introductions and refreshments, Belinda raised the reason for the whole expedition.

'Sir, my father sent me here because he trusted that you would guard some things which are very precious to him until times are safer in England. My aunt has doubtless told you that my father is a collector, especially of small objects made of gold. We have brought the finest specimens from his collection, in the hope that you will take them into your care.'

Unwittingly, she had found the way to the Count's heart. It turned out that he too was an art collector, and was horrified when she told him that her father had feared that his precious objects might be melted down for bullion.

'Of course I will assist a fellow collector!' the Count assured her. 'I shall take pleasure in viewing what your father has sent.' He looked round at all of them. 'Please, regard yourselves as my honoured guests.'

Later they were taken to the rooms that had been prepared for them. Their bedchambers were vast, supplied with everything they could possibly want. No matter how forbidding the outside of the building, the owners obviously insisted on comfort inside. Jane and Belinda took great delight in examining every detail of their rooms and only realised how time was passing when a maid entered, curtseyed, and told them she was there to help them change for dinner.

The gowns she unpacked and laid out for them were very creased, and they were made painfully aware of this when they went down to dinner and discovered that there were two other guests — a gentleman about the same age as Robert, and a lady who was probably near forty but was endeavouring to appear ten years younger.

Monsieur Bellac was handsome, elegant, but also charming. Their first sight of Madame St Claud's elaborate gown, however, made Belinda and Jane feel very dowdy, and the way in which she looked them up and down, eyebrows slightly raised, made them feel worse. But the Count and his wife were very hospitable and after days of eating at inns, the English guests thoroughly enjoyed the meal and their surroundings.

The Count and his guests wanted to know as much as possible about the looming crisis in England, though they found it difficult to believe that the common people would dare turn against their king. They also asked about the journey to Normandy and sat fascinated as details emerged of the dangers Belinda and her friends had faced.

'But thanks to you, Monsieur Hetherington, they are all safe,' commented Madame St Claud, who was clearly taken with Robert. 'You are so very courageous.'

'So were my friends,' he returned. 'This was the first time they had faced danger and they showed great bravery.'

Both guests were very interested in the golden treasure. 'I would very much like to see these beautiful objects,' observed Monsieur Bellac.

'At the moment I have put the chest, unopened, in my strong room,' the Count informed him, 'but I am looking forward to examining the contents tomorrow and you may see everything then.'

The Count noticed Belinda trying to conceal a yawn, and rose to his feet. 'We keep country hours here, mademoiselle. Shall we retire for the night?'

★　★　★

The following morning all seven gentlefolk gathered to see Sir Henry Spence's prized possessions carefully unwrapped and inspected. The two French guests were full of admiration, but it was the Count who was almost silent with wonder, lovingly caressing each piece, from portrait medallions to rare pieces from the Americas that Spanish conquistadors had brought back to Europe.

'These are beautiful,' he said sincerely. 'Your father has done me a great honour by entrusting them to me. I shall be sure to keep them safe for him.'

Monsieur Bellac picked up a small statuette and eyed it curiously.

'These things are very valuable?'

The Count took the statuette from him tenderly.

'Their value is high simply as pure gold, but the age and artistry means that some of them are of incalculable value to a collector.'

Belinda felt a weight had been lifted from her. She could forget the gold now, and simply enjoy herself. That afternoon, as the weather was unusually fine for the time of year, she accompanied her aunt on a walk in the park.

Aunt Maria might have shown little interest in her family for the past fifteen years, separated from them by the Channel and her busy life at the French court, but now she was eager to hear every detail of their lives and those of their neighbours whom she could recall. Simon and Jane had their family histories discussed as well. The reason for this curiosity soon became plain; the Countess was thoroughly bored by country life.

'Everything is so dull!' she complained. 'Nothing ever happens. My husband has his library and his art collection, but what am I supposed to do in the country to amuse myself?'

Belinda thought of her own home life and how the mistresses of the big houses around her conducted their lives. No matter how wealthy their families, the mistress was closely involved in running the house, in keeping an eye on the kitchen and the linen cupboard and deciding what should be served for the meals. She had already realised that the Countess left all such matters to the housekeeper and the butler.

'You have your friends to talk to,' she suggested.

The Countess gave a shrug. 'Monsieur Bellac and Madame St Claud? I invited them because I thought they would amuse me, but although they take full advantage of our hospitality they do not appear to recognise that they should do something for me in return.' She lowered her voice, though even her maid was out of earshot. 'Both of them are short of money. That is why they were willing to leave the court to accompany us to Normandy where we are providing them with free food and lodging, where they have servants to wait on them, and no creditors can pester them.'

Belinda looked at her in surprise.

'They do not look as though they need money.'

'You mean their clothes? They spend what they have on keeping up appearances. Monsieur Bellac obviously hopes to find a wealthy wife who will consider it worth paying for his charm and good looks. Madame St Claud would probably settle for any man who would pay her debts.' She sighed, as though pitying her friend, but managed to look smug at the same time. 'Her husband left her comfortably off when he died but then she fell for a handsome ne'er-do-well who managed to get his hands on most of her fortune before he abandoned her.'

She shivered as a cool breeze rustled the treetops. 'Let us go in, my dear. The weather is getting worse.'

'But your park is beautiful even now,' Belinda told her.

The Countess looked round complacently. 'It is fine enough, I agree, but in a month or two you will see it in its full glory.'

'A month or two?' Belinda echoed. 'But unfortunately I shall be back in England then.'

The Countess shook her head vehemently.

'Nonsense! You are here to visit me, not just to bring your father's collection. I expect you to stay for several weeks at least.'

5

Belinda reported this conversation to Jane and Simon. Simon protested that he would have to leave quite soon, as his parents had not expected him to come to France and would be waiting anxiously for his return.

'I admit I would rather not make the journey on my own. If Master Hetherington is going back soon, I could go with him. Of course, I do not wish to leave you, Belinda.'

'His plans are still vague. Last night he was talking of going to Paris. What about you, Jane?'

'I like it here,' her friend said firmly. 'I think it would be impolite to hurry away too soon.'

Belinda reflected that Jane was well aware that she would probably never experience such a luxurious style of living again. Back in England she would spend her days trying to eke out her father's limited income, often doing domestic work that other families would leave to their servants.

'Very well,' Belinda sighed. 'You and I, Jane, will stay for a month. Simon, you decide when you learn what Master Hetherington has planned.'

In fact, Robert informed them the following day that he had decided to go to Paris so that he could talk with people who would help him form some idea of how the French government would react to Englishmen fighting Englishmen.

'Then will you come back here, or go straight to England?' Simon asked anxiously. Robert shrugged.

'It will make little difference to me, but having brought you all here I feel I should call on my way back so as to be able to take the latest news of the ladies back to their families. If you will wait until then, Simon, we can go back together.'

Simon, looking greatly relieved, said

that he would probably do that.

Belinda was aware that she would miss Robert. There was no doubt that he was stimulating company, and she was not the only one to realise that.

'Madame St Claud seems very taken with you,' she commented to Robert after one dinner when the lady guest had been ogling Robert unashamedly. He lifted an eyebrow.

'Is she? I am afraid she will be disappointed. I do not particularly care for the lady.'

Belinda glanced at him from under lowered lashes.

'Is there any lady you do care for?' she ventured. 'I mean, are you eager to return to Virginia because there is someone waiting for you there?'

He laughed and shook his head. 'No. I have no lady at present.'

'Why ever not? You are well-born, eligible.'

He shrugged. 'I have met some women that I have liked very much, but I have not fallen in love.' He paused, and the black lashes veiled the golden eyes. 'I did think at one time that I had found a special woman whom I could love, but then I discovered that she loved someone else, and was going to marry him.' He stood up abruptly. 'Now, if you will excuse me, I must make preparations. I am leaving for Paris tomorrow.'

Belinda gazed after him, wondering who the special woman had been — and wondering how she would have felt, had she been made aware that Robert Hetherington loved her. Few women would be able to resist him if he set himself to win them, she decided.

Life settled into a comfortable routine once Robert had gone. The three younger guests walked in the park or rode through the countryside and amused themselves with books and various games when the weather was unfavourable. The Countess, who seemed to have few intellectual resources of her own, took part in many of their activities when she was not taking a nap, something she did frequently during the day. Her husband was usually in his library or studying one of the artistic works he had collected. More than once Belinda had found him admiring one or other of her father's golden artefacts, and she hoped that it would not be too great a wrench for him when he eventually had to return them to their owner.

Monsieur Bellac would frequently exercise one the Count's stable of fine horses, or he would sit a little apart from the other guests, apparently regarding their pastimes with slightly condescending amusement. He was obviously practised at flirtation and made some advances to Belinda which she found amusing at first, but then a little annoying. She complained to her aunt, who giggled.

'My dear, he may find you attractive, but I think he finds your father's gold even more so, and you are the heiress to that very desirable treasure.'

'Is that that the reason? Well, I shall make it abundantly clear that I am not interested in him.'

Accordingly, the next time Monsieur Bellac paid her an elaborate compliment, she laughed. 'Did you not say the same thing to Madame St Claud yesterday? I must tell Simon that he should take lessons from you in making pretty speeches.'

After that he kept his flattery for Aunt Maria and Madame St Claud.

Belinda was surprised to find that Simon had developed a strong dislike of Monsieur Bellac.

'Why don't you like him?' she asked curiously after Simon made some disparaging remark. 'He is harmless enough, poor man. Fancy having to be so nice to my aunt just so he may go on enjoying free board and lodging!'

Simon's lips tightened. 'I feel he has an unpleasant streak. You know he asked me if I would like to practise fencing with him the other day, and I agreed? He is obviously an accomplished swordsman, so he treated me easily. All was well at first, and I was grateful for the things he taught me. But then, just once, I managed to penetrate his defence and tap his chest with my foil. After that, he was attacking me without mercy as though it was a real encounter, until I began to fear that he would indeed harm me and I was obliged to tell him I had had enough for the day. I have declined his invitations to practise with him since.'

Belinda grew thoughtful, admitting to herself that once or twice Monsieur Bellac had had a look in his eyes which did not match the role of harmless hanger-on that he was playing.

'And Madame St Claud? What do you think of her?'

Simon was smiling. 'She is very nice to me, poor woman. It is a pity there do not seem to be any suitable husbands for her in Normandy. Fortunately, I am spoken for.' He clasped Belinda's hand.

'It has seemed to me occasionally that she and Monsieur Bellac know each other better than they admit.'

Simon looked at her a little patronisingly. 'And would that shock you? Remember, Belinda, that your experience of society has been limited to the provinces. Life at court is very different.'

Belinda did not reply, though she was tempted to say something which would have upset his complacency. After all, he had spent precisely two weeks in London with his father the previous year, which scarcely made him an authority on court manners. She was coming to realise that he had little interest or curiosity about matters which did not affect him directly, and that his attitudes and beliefs were borrowed from his father and friends rather than being the result of his own thoughts. Could she happily spend decades of marriage with someone with such limited intellectual interests?

Then she told herself not to be silly. Simon was well-born and would inherit a good estate. He was also presentable, honourable and in love with her. In any case, married couples did not normally spend as much time together as she and Simon were doing at present. When they were married Simon would be busy managing the estate, or engaged in hunting and other masculine pursuits, while she would be running the house and looking after their children. She was betrothed to Simon now, so there was nothing she could do. The betrothal might be informal, but the whole of their acquaintanceship knew that it existed.

Once or twice when she did snap at Simon for some reason, he took shelter in Jane's undemanding companionship. Jane obviously admired him greatly and this clearly flattered his ego, so they got on very well together.

Belinda found herself looking forward to Robert Hetherington's return. This came unexpectedly when he and his servant came riding to the castle on a grey day when rain was sweeping across the countryside. It could not have been the weather alone, however, which accounted for his dour look or his lack of formal greeting when he met her in the hall.

'Is the Count in his library?' he asked urgently, and when Belinda confirmed this he strode away without another word and was closeted with the Count for some time, emerging with him to announce the grim news to the rest of the party.

'We heard in Paris that a few days ago, His Majesty King Charles called on the governor of Hull to admit him to the town and surrender to him a store of arms and ammunition which lay there. The governor shut the gates and answered that he took orders only from Parliament. The king has ordered all trustworthy gentlemen to muster men in his name, and Parliament are recruiting more men for their army. It is only a matter of time before hostilities begin.' He drew his hand over his face as if wiping away a veil of despair. 'Before, there was always a hope that good sense would prevail and civil war could be averted, but now bloodshed is inevitable.'

'Will France become involved?' Belinda's aunt asked nervously, and was obviously relieved when he shook his head.

'Not openly, not directly. You know that Charles's queen, Henrietta Maria, is the French king's sister, but, as you also know, France has problems of its own.' He turned to the three English guests. 'The French queen, Anne of Austria, has produced two sons after twenty-three childless years, but her husband is not in good health. If he were to die Anne would become Regent of France with her infant son as Louis the fourteenth. There are many rival factions at court, none of whom want a war with England.'

'What happens now?' Jane inquired timidly.

'I return to England in a few days. Simon, you wish to accompany me?'

Before Simon could answer, Belinda interrupted.

'I will come with you as well. I must

return to my father before fighting starts and it becomes too dangerous to travel. Do you agree, Jane?'

Jane nodded, and Robert sighed. 'Very well. I still have to visit some gentlemen in this area, so we will leave in a few days.'

'We shall miss you all,' said the Count heavily, and this was echoed politely by Monsieur Bellac and Madame St Claud, who had listened in silence to Robert's announcement. After all, the war would have little or no effect on them, but when Belinda and her friends had left, her aunt would once more be reliant on them for company.

However, to everyone's surprise Monsieur Bellac announced that he would be leaving the next day, called back to Paris by personal affairs. No one was aware of his having received any messages recently, but perhaps country life — even when it cost him nothing — was proving too boring for him and the 'message' was simply a polite excuse to leave.

Afterwards Aunt Maria called Belinda

to speak to her in private. The countess seemed unusually serious, but took some time to come to the point. Finally, taking Belinda's hands in her own, she blurted out, 'My dear, don't go back to England. Stay here with me.'

Belinda stared at her. 'But my father will be expecting me.'

'Write to him saying that you are happy here.' As Belinda hesitated, her aunt went on. 'Point out to him that you will be safer here than in England. My husband says that as soon as fighting starts in England, there will be a flood of refugees coming to France to find shelter. You are welcome to stay with us for as long as you like.'

'Aunt Maria, you are very kind, but my father needs me at home. Heaven knows what a mess the house and stores will be in when I get there!'

'But I need you!' cried her aunt. 'I'm lonely, and no one needs me here. My husband is fond of me, but his scholarly interests take up most of his time and I cannot share them. If only you knew how I long for a child! It would give my life a purpose, someone to love who would need me. But after fifteen childless years there seems little chance of that.'

Belinda's arms were round her aunt, trying to comfort her.

'I shall always be grateful for the way you welcomed us when we arrived without warning, and I shall try to come again, but I must go back to England now.'

Her aunt's eyes were full of tears. 'I could take you to Paris, to the court,' she said desperately. 'You would love it there.'

'And what about Simon?'

Her aunt shrugged. 'You do not really care about Simon. Anyone can see that. You could find a better husband in Paris.'

Belinda was silent, trying to think what to say. Finally she took a deep breath. 'It is my duty to go back to England, Aunt Maria.'

Her aunt heard the note of finality in

her niece's voice and fought for self-control, dabbing her eyes with a lace-trimmed handkerchief. At last she managed a watery smile.

'Of course you must go then, my dear. I was merely being selfish.'

As Belinda hovered over her anxiously she gave a half-laugh.

'Go now, and leave me alone. I just need a few minutes by myself.'

Belinda left the room, closing the door gently behind her, and started down the main staircase. In the hall below, she saw Robert listening to the Count, who was obviously extremely agitated. As Belinda reached the bottom of the stairs they became aware of her presence and turned to her.

'What is the matter?' she demanded.

The Count was grey-faced. 'Your father's treasure has been stolen,' he told her despairingly.

Belinda looked at him with disbelief, then Robert, but he shook his head.

'The Count has not explained to me yet.'

Taking the older man by the arm, he led him to a chair. The Count collapsed into it and gazed up at them in despair.

'You remember, Monsieur Hetherington, that I was in my library looking at some of the Italian portrait medallions — six of them — when you arrived, and when we went out to tell everyone your news I left the medallions on my desk. I admit I forgot about them but I had no reason to think they would not be safe. When I went back about half an hour ago, the medallions had gone! I thought at first that my servant had put them away, but he says no.'

'Do you believe him?' asked Robert, and the Count nodded.

'He has been in my service since he was a boy and I trust him, as I trust all the servants who have access to my library.'

Robert was pacing the floor, his hands behind his back.

'You could have their belongings searched,' he began, but the Count interrupted him.

'No! They would not have done such a thing, and, anyway, there would be no point. If anyone tried to sell such precious things within twenty miles of here I would soon learn of it.'

Robert's eyes narrowed. 'There is someone else,' he said slowly, 'someone in desperate need of money who could sell such objects in Paris without raising too many questions, someone who could swear that they were family heirlooms he was forced to part with.'

'Monsieur Bellac?' breathed Belinda, and then nodded. 'He and Madame St Claud were the last to arrive when you were telling us the news from England. If he went into the library and saw the medallions lying there, he could easily have taken them before he joined us.'

'And then he announced his unexpected departure,' added Robert. He whirled round to the Count. 'When is he leaving?'

'Early tomorrow morning,' said the Count heavily.

'But surely if he had taken the medallions he would have gone by now,' Belinda argued. 'He would know that you would find they had gone and might suspect him.'

The Count's smile was a ghastly grimace. 'He also knows that if I accuse him of theft, I will be questioning his honour.'

'So?' Belinda looked bemused.

'So he will be entitled to defend his honour by challenging me to a duel.'

Belinda remembered what Simon had said about Monsieur Bellac's skill as a swordsman. 'But you have gout! You could not fight him.'

Both men looked at her as if she had said something particularly stupid.

'I could not refuse to fight him, to give him satisfaction,' the Count said simply. 'It would dishonour me. And then he would kill me.'

'That is ridiculous!' she said hotly. 'Robert, tell him that is nonsense.'

But Robert shook his head heavily. Then he turned slowly to the Count, a slow smile curling his mouth. 'Perhaps there is a way of getting the medallions back without Bellac knowing.'

The other two looked at him eagerly.

'The medallions are probably safe under lock and key somewhere in his room, wrapped to protect them. If we can substitute objects of a similar size and weight without him knowing, all will be well. If he examines what he has before he leaves and finds that we have substituted rubbish, he cannot accuse us of taking the medallions without revealing that he is a thief. Most probably he will not be aware that his hoard has been replaced and he will ride away in the morning unaware that he has lost the gold.'

Hope was dawning on the Count's face.

'I could keep him talking in the library for some time if I asked him to take some messages to friends in Paris. But how can we gain access to his room to find where he has hidden the medallions without leaving any trace that would warn him?'

Robert was grinning. 'That will not be a problem. My servant Harry has certain unusual skills. If you can draw Monsieur Bellac away, I will keep watch while Harry searches the room and then I will come to the library as a signal that we have finished.' He looked thoughtful. 'You said that Monsieur Bellac and Madame St Claud came in together when I was telling you the news of England. She might have been with him when he took the medallions, though I do not believe he would let any of them out of his possession. Can she be distracted as well?'

Half an hour later Belinda saw Monsieur Bellac, wearing a slightly irritated frown, follow the servant who had summoned him into the library. She hovered nearby, casting glances up the staircase and straining to hear Robert's footsteps, which would assure her all was well. The Countess, unquestioningly following her husband's instructions, had asked Madame

105

St Claud to help her disentangle a complicated piece of embroidery.

Time passed, then to Belinda's horror the library door opened and Monsieur Bellac strode out. The Count's voice could be heard, obviously trying to detain him further, but his guest shut the door behind him and was making for the staircase, for his room. He had to be stopped!

Quickly Belinda darted out of the corner where she had been lurking and called out to the hastening figure, 'Monsieur Bellac!'

Politeness compelled him to stop, though he was clearly irritated at the interruption. 'Mademoiselle?'

What reason could she give for keeping him there? She laid a hand on his arm. 'I have been hoping to have a private word with you.'

What about? She thought furiously, and then smiled up at him.

'I wanted to say goodbye, to tell you that I shall miss you.'

He lifted his eyebrows. 'You have not

appeared to want my company.'

Belinda actually managed a giggle. 'It was difficult — Simon was always nearby — but I have been aware of you.'

Now Monsieur Bellac was smiling in his turn. He was accustomed to being able to charm women easily, and Belinda's apparent indifference had stung his pride. His arm went round her waist and she forced herself not to shrink away, but instead lifted her face to his. He bent to kiss her — but at that moment they heard a heavy tread coming down the stairs and hastily separated. Robert appeared, gave them a cheerful nod as he passed, and made his way to the library.

Freed from Bellac's hold, Belinda picked up her skirts and fled.

6

Belinda made her way into the garden where she stood, eyes closed, gulping in the fresh air, trying to calm herself.

'You look flushed, Belinda.'

It was Simon, and he was looking at her very coldly. She put her hands to her face. 'It was hot indoors.'

'Indeed? Monsieur Bellac's embrace must have warmed you as well.'

She looked at him, at a loss for words, as he went on. 'I saw you stop him and clearly invite him to hold you!'

Belinda was about to tell him that she had been desperate to stop Bellac finding Robert and Harry in his room, then realised that if she did so, Simon would know that once again she had not confided in him.

'It was just a harmless flirtation,' she said lamely.

'Did it not occur to you that as my

promised wife, you are not supposed to flirt with other men?'

He turned on his heel and strode away, and Robert found her still standing there when he came looking for her five minutes later.

'What's the matter?' he said when he saw her upset face.

'I've quarrelled with Simon. He saw Bellac embracing me. I was only trying to stop him interrupting you and Harry, but I could not tell Simon why I had behaved like that.'

'I hope not! He would feel duty bound to challenge Bellac to a duel, just after we have averted one!'

'I will make up with him later. What did you find?'

He smiled triumphantly. 'The medallions were in a small chest, wrapped in cloth. Harry replaced them with bits of iron from the stable and relocked the chest without leaving the slightest sign that he had been there.'

'Were those the unusual skills you were talking about? How did you know he could do that?'

He grimaced. 'I met Harry in Virginia. He had been transported there as a thief, a very successful thief who only escaped the gallows because the Virginian landowners were desperate for workers. I found out that he had a genius for dealing with even the most complicated locks and leaving no trace of what he had done.'

'But he must have been caught, or he would not have been transported,' Belinda pointed out.

'He does not deal with women so well. His sweetheart found that he was visiting another woman, and, worse, giving her gifts of jewellery — things that he had stolen — and out of jealousy she betrayed him to the authorities. In Virginia I took him hunting from time to time and got to know him well. He's a good servant, glad to have escaped work on the plantations as well as hanging.' He laughed. 'But I never thought I would ask him to use his burglary skills on my behalf!'

110

He put a comforting arm round her shoulders. 'Come inside now. It is going to rain. Do not worry about Simon. You did well to distract Bellac.'

Belinda turned gratefully towards him in the shelter of his arm and rested her hands on his breast like a child. For a moment he tensed, and then his arms went round her tightly and as she looked up at him in surprise he bent his head to kiss her, her mouth opening at the touch of his lips. She was aware of the feel of his body, and the way her own body responded with sensations she had never experienced before. Then suddenly she panicked and struggled to be free. He released her abruptly and stepped back.

'Forgive me!' he said. 'I should not have done that, not when I know you belong to Simon Gregory. But you have been so brave, so courageous . . . '

Her heart was thudding, but she shook her head.

'Perhaps my actions misled you and you misinterpreted my feelings, my gratitude. Let us forget it happened,' she told him. 'It was a reaction to the excitement, to the danger — that is all.'

They went indoors without another word and Belinda went to her room, pleading a headache due to the stress of the past hours when the Countess tried to speak to her. There, curled up in an armchair, she willed herself to relax. The unexpected embrace had meant nothing, she told herself, but she remembered very clearly the warmth of Robert's body, and how the passion of his kiss had been quite unlike Simon's chaste embraces.

She frowned when she thought of Simon and his displeasure, but she had to reconcile herself with him, so she found her way downstairs to the pleasant little drawing-room where they spent much of their time. He was there with Jane, and one reproachful look from Jane made Belinda immediately aware that Simon had told her friend all about her disgraceful behaviour with Bellac.

Endeavouring to appear meekly repentant, Belinda asked Jane if she would leave her alone with Simon for a short while. After their friend had gone Simon stood by the fireplace, his face set. Belinda felt a surge of impatience. She had only done what she had to do! His tender sensibilities, this display of wounded dignity, were just a nuisance. Outwardly, however, she smiled at him and held out her hands.

'I'm sorry, Simon. I didn't mean to lead Monsieur Bellac on, and when he took hold of me I didn't know what to do.'

Faced with a repentant Belinda, Simon melted rapidly. Soon he was pointing out that an inexperienced young girl like Belinda was always at a disadvantage with a man like Bellac.

'When you are more experienced, you will know how to handle men like that,' he informed her, while Belinda privately thought that she had handled Bellac very well — almost as well as she was handling Simon now.

Dinner was a quiet meal that night. Robert sat by Madame St Claud and said little. One guest did not appear, to the relief of several people. The count announced that Monsieur Bellac had decided to ride through the night and had, in fact, already left.

Madame St Claud turned to Robert. 'I understand you will be leaving the day after tomorrow, Monsieur Hetherington. So shall I. Indeed, I shall be most grateful if you will let me go with your party as far as Arras.' She turned to Belinda's aunt. 'I am most grateful for your hospitality, my dear, but I feel I have imposed myself on you long enough. A friend of mine is returning to Paris, and I received a message from her today inviting me to meet her in Arras so we can return to the court together. The message was waiting for me after I left you.'

Aunt Maria was looking distressed.

'But that means you will all have

gone! I shall be left alone!' She caught her husband's eye. 'Except for you, my dear, of course.'

The invitation to Madame St Claud seemed too opportune to be true, but Robert confirmed its existence later. Belinda had by then convinced herself that the incident in the garden had been a momentary aberration, as much her fault as his; one which need not spoil their friendship. When Belinda found an opportunity to confer with Robert, he informed her that he had checked and a message had indeed been delivered to Madame St Claud.

'Of course, we only have her word for it that the message is from a lady friend. It might well be from Monsieur Bellac, arranging for her to join him.'

'Which would mean that he has not yet discovered he has a load of worthless iron instead of the gold?'

'Exactly! Let us hope he remains in ignorance until he and Madame St Claud are reunited.'

That night, at bedtime, Jane came to

Belinda's room. Belinda, chatting casually, glanced round at her friend on receiving no reply to some question and saw tears rolling down her cheeks. She dropped the garment she had been folding.

'My dear! What's the matter?'

Jane shook her head dismally. 'I do not want to go home! I like it here! Life is so comfortable and so easy, and I do not have to do anything unless I wish to. I can live like a gentlewoman.' She held out her hands. 'Look! They are white and soft, as a gentlewoman's hands should be, but at home they are always red and rough with housework.'

Belinda held Jane in her arms, trying to comfort her but knowing there was really nothing she could do.

'Aunt Maria desires a companion. Perhaps you could stay with her?' she suggested, but Jane shook her head.

'She wants someone lively and pretty — like you. And it is my duty to look after my father — at least, that is what he always says.'

'Well, it will be a few days yet before we are back home. We can enjoy the journey with Robert and Simon.'

Jane nodded. 'Simon has been very kind to me.' She managed a smile. 'I am just being selfish, Belinda, but I will always look back on our time in France with great pleasure, in spite of the awful journey here.'

Belinda's own feelings about the return home were mixed. Unlike Jane, she would be going back to a comfortable house and a prosperous estate, but she was beginning to think that it would seem very dull after the last few weeks. She also had growing doubts about her relationship with Simon. Their travels together seemed to have emphasised their differences rather than bringing them closer. However, they were committed to going home and she would be needed there, so there was no point in worrying about it.

Their departure, unlike their arrival, was made in some style. The Count insisted on sending an escort of four of his grooms with them, and the Countess anxiously interrogated the party to make sure they had everything they would need.

Belinda had grown to respect the Count and said goodbye to him reluctantly, but she was near to tears as she embraced her aunt. In spite of what they said, they both knew that it was most unlikely they would ever see each other again.

'You know how sorry I am to see you go. I think my husband's health means that we shall spend little time in Paris from now on, so if you wish to come back here again, because you need a refuge or just for a visit, I shall greet you like a daughter.'

But the parting was inevitable, Robert and Simon were growing impatient, and finally the party set off, after Madame St Claud had assured her 'dear, dear friend' that she would write frequently with all the news of the court.

The journey went very smoothly.

This time Belinda and Jane rode on each side of Simon while the French-woman rode with Robert. When they arrived at Arras Madame St Claud allowed them to escort her to the bustling inn where she was supposed to rendezvous with her friend. There was no sign of the friend, but Madame St Claud refused all their offers to wait there until her arrival.

'Nonsense! I know Germaine. She will be here soon, so I will just rest here till she comes. You must not allow me to delay you.'

Robert insisted on arranging that Madame St Claud should have a private room to wait in and that suitable refreshments would be provided. They saw her safely installed there, together with her surprisingly small amount of luggage, and then they took their leave of her.

'What do you think will happen to her?' Belinda asked Robert quietly as they prepared to remount.

'Perhaps this Germaine actually exists

and will take her to Paris. Perhaps Monsieur Bellac will arrive. However, most likely the gentleman will have abandoned Madame St Claud and she will wait, but nobody will appear.'

'What will she do then?'

'She might arrange to be taken back to your aunt's, though it would be difficult to explain why her friend had not appeared. But I think Madame St Claud will somehow persuade a traveller with a spare seat in his coach to take her to Paris. But do not worry about her. I am certain she will survive — at someone else's expense.'

At this moment Belinda chanced to look round casually at the bystanders, and so it was she who first saw the man with the drawn sword charging across the yard towards Robert. She screamed, Robert turned sharply towards her, and the first sword slash missed him by inches. The attacker was Monsieur Bellac, lips drawn back in a snarl, heedless of onlookers, and intent only on killing his defenceless enemy.

With a vague idea of coming to Robert's aid, Belinda snatched a short staff from a bystander, but before she could decide how to use it, Robert called to her.

'Give it me!' he said urgently. She threw the primitive weapon to him before Bellac could strike again. Robert caught it and desperately parried the next stroke, but the staff was not long enough to keep Bellac at bay and he was lunging forward rapidly, trying to stab Robert before he could bring the staff into play again. The fight was brutish but short, over before any of the onlookers could interfere further. Robert twisted to avoid the blade and risked leaving himself exposed briefly so as to give himself a chance to bring the staff up hard against Bellac's head. The Frenchman reeled from the blow and Robert hit him again, harder, sending him to the ground. Then Robert's boot pinned down Bellac's sword, tearing it from his hand, and Robert seized his attacker's shirt front, pulling him towards him.

There was no trace left of the Count's charming guest now. He was sweating, furious and full of hate.

'You took them!' he spat at Robert. 'I know not how, but you did!'

Robert's grip tightened. 'What did I take? Tell me, now, in front of these witnesses, and brand yourself a thief!'

Monsieur Bellac's eyes rolled round and he saw the eager audience surrounding them, with Harry now holding his own sword perilously near his neck. Suddenly he seemed to realise how hopeless his situation was, for he groaned and collapsed limply. Robert let him fall to the ground where he sat, his head in his hands. Robert stood with his hands on his hips and looked down at him contemptuously.

'You've lost everything, Bellac. Go away and find some hole to hide in.'

Bellac climbed to his feet, grey-faced and weary, turned, and began to trudge towards the arch of the inn's courtyard.

Suddenly there was a cry of 'Etienne!' and Madame St Claud ran from the inn door and seized his arm. He pushed her away without even looking at her and vanished from sight. Madame St Claud stared after him, tears streaming down her face. Robert approached her.

'Madame,' he said, 'let him go. There is no future for you with him. There is a coach leaving for Paris in an hour. Be on it. I shall pay for your journey. Go back to the friends you still have in Paris.'

At first she did not seem to have heard him, and it was Belinda who came forward to lead the distraught woman back to the private room and help her compose herself so that when the Paris coach was ready to leave she was able to board it with some dignity, to face whatever the future held.

Finally the others could set out on their journey again.

Jane and Simon were clearly bewildered by the incident.

'Why did Monsieur Bellac attack

Master Hetherington, and what was he talking about?' Jane asked, but no one answered.

Simon edged closer to Belinda. 'You knew all about it, whatever it was,' he murmured accusingly. When she did not reply, he moved away from her and stayed near Jane for the rest of the day.

★ ★ ★

The journey passed without further incident and they crossed the Channel on a comfortable French merchant vessel, landing at Dover on a perfect June day. Once back on English soil, they were soon aware of subtle changes. People seemed wary of strangers and far more men went armed or in full military array. There were rumours about who had declared for Parliament and who was for the king. Not all the aristocracy had chosen the Royalist side. Thirty years earlier King Charles' father, James, had forced through the divorce of the Earl and Countess of

Essex so that his favourite, the Earl of Somerset, could marry the countess. Now the Earl of Essex took his revenge, becoming supreme commander of the forces of Parliament.

Robert's duty was to return to his brother and give his news of France, but not before he and Harry had seen his three charges all safely home. Simon's parents welcomed their son with open arms and even Jane's father had apparently realised during her absence how dependent he was on her. Belinda's feelings were mixed as she saw her own home appear. It would give her safety and security and reassure her that violence and theft were temporary aberrations in her life, but it would also mean a farewell to adventure — and to Robert Hetherington — and she was beginning to realise how much she would miss him.

Once he had seen her happy reunion with her father, Robert refused all offers of rest and refreshment.

'I must get to Ruthington as soon as I

can,' he excused himself, standing in the entrance hall.

'I shall miss you,' Belinda said simply.

He smiled at her, and then glanced around. Her father had gone to fetch a letter, which he wanted Robert to deliver to the earl, leaving the two of them momentarily alone.

'Let us say goodbye properly,' Robert said suddenly, and when he stretched out his arms to her she went to him willingly. This time his embrace was strong but gentle. She responded with instinctive passion to his kiss and then they stood unmoving, his face buried in her hair.

'I shall always remember you, Belinda, even if we never meet again,' he murmured huskily.

For a moment longer they clung to each other, only to separate hastily as they heard her father returning.

'I shall be most grateful if you will give your brother this,' said Sir Henry, handing him the letter.

'It will be no trouble,' Robert

answered mechanically, his eyes never leaving Belinda's face as she stared at him wide-eyed, hardly believing what had happened.

He left without another word, bowing briefly to Belinda. She watched him ride away with Harry until a bend in the drive hid them from sight.

7

For Belinda to resume the life she had left when she went to France was not so easy. The day-to-day routine was much the same, but it was more difficult than usual to obtain many things needed for the house because there were fewer merchants travelling the country. She was also dismayed by the news that John, the groom, and his brother had escaped from prison before they could be tried.

Some acquaintances were now cold-shouldered because they had chosen to support Parliament. Her own immediate circle of friends was unchanged, but their attitudes to each other were different. At first Lydia Somers wanted to know everything about Belinda's grand French relatives, but once she had learned all there was to know about the castle and the ladies' French fashions she could talk of nothing but the young Royalist officers she had met.

Belinda had believed that the experiences she shared with Jane would have forged a bond between them, but Jane seemed to be avoiding her.

That left Simon. He was naturally caught up in the preparations for war and was busy practising the use of weapons and studying military strategy with other young Royalists of the area. Even so, Belinda felt he could have come to see her more often, and when he did visit he seemed preoccupied and distant. She knew he had not always been pleased with her behaviour during their adventures, but was that enough to make him forget that she was still the prettiest heiress in the area — still the girl with whom he had fallen in love?

One Sunday after church Belinda's father fell into conversation with Simon, Belinda occasionally interjecting a remark. Simon, however, seemed distracted, his attention elsewhere. He was looking beyond Belinda, and when she casually turned her head, she realised he was looking at Jane — who was gazing back at him, sadness and longing on her face. When Belinda turned back, she saw the same emotions in Simon's eyes.

That night she lay awake for hours. Simon and Jane were in love; there was no doubt about that. The two of them had been thrown closely together during their stay in France; that had given Simon a chance to get to know Jane well and to appreciate her qualities, while Belinda knew that Jane had always admired Simon. And it could not be denied that on more than one occasion, they had been drawn together by their mutual disapproval of some action of Belinda's.

So, what should be done now? Belinda was betrothed to Simon, a state almost as binding as marriage; he could not break off their engagement with honour, or without shaming Belinda. She had no doubt that if she did nothing, he would feel obliged to marry her. She was also sure that he would make her a good husband and that she would be able to keep him contented enough most of the time so that he would not pine too much for his unacknowledged lost love, Jane.

She did not think for a minute that Jane had considered the possibility that Simon might marry her instead of Belinda. In fact she would probably refuse to have anything to do with him if he tried to break his word to her friend. The sensible thing would be to say nothing; to try to forget the looks that had passed between Jane and Simon, to marry him whenever it was convenient, and devote herself to housekeeping and motherhood.

But did she wish to do that? Did she wish to make her friends unhappy? That was one point. Another, even more important: did she still wish to marry Simon? She recalled the number of times she had found Simon irritating or frankly boring, and had turned instead to Robert Hetherington for action and stimulation. Her trip to France might have involved danger, but it had given her a glimpse of the wider world and its possibilities.

She remembered the captain of The Pelican talking about his voyages across the ocean, and how Robert had talked of birds and animals that no one in England had ever seen. As soon as she married Simon, her horizons would narrow forever to the little world she already knew.

But what else could she do? At the moment she was in the worst possible situation — neither free nor married.

She fell asleep at last, and woke to find that her subconscious mind had decided for her while she was sleeping.

★ ★ ★

Simon had told her when he would be calling next, and she took great care over her appearance that day. Her hair was carefully arranged, and she wore her most becoming gown. She greeted him warmly when he arrived, held his arm as they walked in the garden, and smiled up at him tenderly.

'Let us sit here,' she said as they passed a bench in a secluded corner. 'There is something I wish to discuss with you, Simon.'

When they were seated, she turned, took both his hands in hers and gazed into his eyes.

'Simon, I know we agreed that we would not marry until the country is at peace once more, but now everybody says that the conflict may go on for years, and I don't want to wait that long. Let us get married — soon!'

For a long moment she saw panic in his eyes, and then he swallowed deeply. 'If that is what you want, Belinda.'

She laughed abruptly and stood up, tearing her hands free.

'It is not what I want, Simon, and neither do you.'

He stood up to face her, bewildered. 'But you said . . . '

'I was testing you, and you failed. Perhaps you once loved me and wanted to marry me — but now you love someone else far more.'

He did not try to deny it.

'But I have asked you to marry me,' he stammered. 'I cannot go back on that now!'

'But *I* can! We were never formally betrothed, which makes it easier. We will let it be known that I decided to break it off, that I changed my mind. People will think me giddy and foolish, but it will give us our freedom. Then, after a suitable time, you can ask Jane to marry you.'

His relief was very obvious and not at all flattering as he tried to thank her. Belinda grimaced.

'Try not to sound so *eager*, Simon.'

He flushed red. 'I am sorry. I did love you, I really did. But then when we were together I got to know Jane well, and one day I realised I was in love with her.' He hesitated. 'I have never told her I love her, because I felt honour-bound to marry you. Do you really think she loves me?'

'Of course she does!' Now her smile was genuine. She felt free.

'Let us be good friends, Simon. That is better than being an unhappy married couple.'

They agreed that she would tell her father that she had decided she did not wish to marry Simon after all, and that he would inform his parents of her decision. They sat chatting together for some time and realised that they felt much more at ease with each other now they were not committed to marriage. At last it was time for him to go. They rose, and he took her hands, smiling down at her with genuine warmth.

'Thank you, Belinda,' he said gratefully, and kissed her for the last time. As she watched him walk away, she compared his polite peck to Robert's passion, and reflected ruefully that men only seemed to kiss her when they were leaving her.

She did not mention Jane when she told her father what she had done, and was surprised by how angry he was.

'He was the perfect match for you, and you have sent him away because of some childish romantic whim!'

'We did not love each other.'

'What does that matter? How many couples at our level of society marry for love? Send after him. Tell him you have changed your mind.'

'It's too late, and in any case I do not wish to. I thought you would want me to be happy.'

Her father looked older, almost haggard. 'I do. That is why I wanted you married to someone like Simon. You have no one apart from me and my sister in France. What would happen to you in these troubled times if I died? You need security, and Simon and his family would have given you that.'

Belinda bowed her head, almost in tears.

'Father, you talk as though I have to be looked after by others and cannot decide anything for myself!'

'You are a young unmarried woman in a country which is about to go to war. What can you decide about your fate?'

'I can decide not to marry Simon!' she flashed angrily, and then shrugged. 'Please, Father, let's not argue about it. What's done is done. I don't think there will be any trouble, but please support me.'

Belinda won him round with difficulty, and hoped devoutly that there would be no complications. She resolved to stay at home for the next few days to give time for word to spread and the inevitable gossip to die down.

⋆　⋆　⋆

A week later Belinda was invited to go to the Somers' house to view some silks that Lady Somers had received from London. She decided this would be a good opportunity to see how the local gentry had reacted to her broken betrothal. Belinda deliberately arrived a little late and was aware of a sudden hush when she was ushered into the room where a number of ladies were admiring the fabrics. Then people began to talk again hurriedly, but they did not look at her. Lydia Somers came forward to greet her.

'Welcome, Belinda! I was afraid you might not come.'

Belinda smiled sweetly and lifted her eyebrows enquiringly.

'Why should I not?'

'Well, we have all heard that Simon has broken off your betrothal.'

'No — it was I who broke it off!' Belinda said sharply.

Lydia giggled. 'Really? That is surprising — in view of the circumstances — but I suppose you have to say it.'

Belinda was determined not to get involved in discussing the matter any further and looked around.

'I can't see Jane. Isn't she coming?'

'We thought it best not to invite both of you.'

'Why on earth not?'

Lydia stared at her with evident surprise and then smiled with malicious delight. 'But my dear Belinda . . . Haven't you heard? Jane and Simon were formally betrothed three days ago — two days after you supposedly *decided* to break your engagement.'

Belinda was lost for words and Lydia saw her evident discomfiture.

'Oh, my poor dear! We all thought it was a bit soon, but Simon's mother said they were so much in love that they couldn't bear to wait any longer!'

'Then I wish them every happiness,' Belinda declared, moving away abruptly towards the rest of the little gathering. She forced herself to look at the silks, exchanged careful small talk with the other ladies, and then left, saying she had business to attend to at home.

Once back in the sanctuary of her own room she was able to let out her anger, pounding her fists on the cushions and weeping tears of fury. Surely Simon had understood that some time would have to elapse before he could ask Jane to marry him? As it was, no matter what Belinda or even

Simon said, no one would now believe that it had been Belinda who had dismissed him. The whole neighbourhood would see her as rejected and unwanted, and all the young men would be wondering what was wrong with her, and why the quiet and not particularly rich or pretty Jane had been preferred to her.

After a day's brooding, she resolved to grasp the nettle and set out to visit Jane — unsure as she was how to confront her. Would she be openly angry, or show hurt dignity? As it was, when an anxious maidservant ushered her into the morning-room where Jane was sewing, Jane took one look at her and burst into tears, and Belinda found herself comforting the girl she had come to challenge.

'I didn't mean to cause you trouble,' sobbed Jane. 'It was just that when Simon told me he loved me and wanted to marry me, I was so proud and happy that I wanted to tell everyone as soon as I could.'

'Of course you did,' soothed Belinda, secretly reflecting that even such a nice girl as Jane must have enjoyed telling the world that Simon preferred her to Belinda. 'The only trouble is that Lydia Somers is gloating over me, and I do so detest that.'

At that moment the door opened and Simon entered hurriedly. The maid had told him that Mistress Spence was already with Jane, so he had clearly hastened to defend his new love against his old, and was disconcerted to be greeted by a smile from Belinda. Jane burst into fresh tears and threw herself into his protective embrace.

'Peace, Simon, I have not come to reproach either of you,' Belinda said patiently. 'However, I spent a highly uncomfortable couple of hours the other day with a group of women who were all pitying me and I do not wish to repeat that.'

'But what can we do?' Jane wailed.

'We can comport ourselves just as we did in France. We can be three good friends. If people see us together, enjoying one another's company, it should become clear that Simon did not leave me against my will, and that I wish you both well — as indeed I do.' She seated herself on a sofa, patting the space next to her. 'Now, let us all sit down and discuss matters.'

By the time Belinda left, it had been arranged that they should be seen together at church on Sunday, and that she and Jane, escorted by Simon, would call on Lady Somers to ask whether Jane could view the silks. On the way home, Belinda was well satisfied with the way things had gone. She also could not resist wondering whether Simon had noticed that crying made Jane's nose red as well as her eyes.

The succeeding days were not the happiest of Belinda's life. Admittedly she enjoyed the half-heard gossip and speculation and the expression on Lydia Somers' face when she saw Simon with both Jane and Belinda, all three apparently happy together, but spending time in public with the other two soon grew wearisome. She decided that Jane burst into tears far too readily, and grew tired of Simon when he persisted in praising Jane and saying how happy he was going to be with her without remembering always to thank Belinda for the freedom which made the happiness possible.

Meanwhile, the rumour of imminent hostilities between the forces of the king and those of Parliament grew ever stronger, and she was not altogether surprised when Jane and Simon decided to marry as soon as they could.

'If the King calls me to arms, then I must go,' Simon said, trying to look noble and soldierly, 'but at least we will be married and Jane will be part of my family. They will care for her, whatever happens to me.'

Jane was bemused with happiness. She turned to Belinda for advice on clothes and how to arrange her hair, and Belinda helped her to ready herself for the ceremony on her wedding day.

She dressed Jane's hair in soft ringlets, insisted her friend wore a blue gown of a shade far more flattering than the ornate gown Jane favoured, and lent her some of her own jewels.

When Jane looked in the mirror, her eyes grew wide.

'I look pretty!' she said in amazement.

'You look beautiful,' Belinda told her. 'Wait until Simon sees you!'

Jane impulsively embraced her friend. 'I should be helping you on *your* wedding day! Instead, thanks to you, I am the bride.' She hesitated. 'Are you sure you don't regret giving up Simon?'

Belinda kissed her. 'No, Jane. He is a very nice young man, but we were not suited. However, I know the two of you will be very happy together.' Jane still looked uncertain, and Belinda laughed. 'Don't worry. Some poor, unsuspecting man somewhere is doomed to become my bridegroom, but Simon has had a lucky escape.'

The celebrations were muted in

comparison to what they would have been in other times. There had been little time for preparation, and many of the gentlemen who would normally be present had already ridden off to serve the king, taking able-bodied menservants with them. The wives and mothers they had left behind were in no mood for jollity.

The older men were talking of war, not of weddings. Already it was clear that money for weapons and wages for soldiers was all-important. Apparently the king had sent his wife across the Channel with his crown jewels and all the money he had been able to raise, and had bid her spend it all in buying arms in France and Holland.

Belinda, passing among the guests, caught a familiar name. 'Did you mention Master Hetherington?' she asked Sir Andrew Somers.

He nodded. 'His Majesty King Charles is sending out commissions of array to every county, to raise men for his cause. Master Hetherington is leading one of the commissions.'

Belinda was thinking as much of Robert as of the newly-weds on her way home with her father. Robert had been sent to her part of the country before. Perhaps she would see him again, if only for a short time. She found herself longing to see his tall figure again, and grew angry with herself. He would not have attached any importance to a couple of snatched kisses.

During the next couple of weeks, the pace of change accelerated. Some servants decided that a military life serving the king would be more exciting than continuing to work for Sir Henry, who felt morally bound to equip them with the arms they required before letting them go. Others favoured Parliament and slipped quietly away, often helping themselves to property they thought might be useful. Horses vanished overnight from the stables.

The result was that Belinda and her father were left with a skeleton staff to run the house and estate. Work on the home farm was reduced to a minimum; it appeared few crops would be planted or harvested that year.

As the life he had known since birth crumbled around him, Sir Henry grew morose. His early military enthusiasm had vanished as he realised no one would want the services of an elderly gentleman, inexperienced in fighting. Belinda tried to remain cheerful and bolster his spirits, but more than once he accused her of causing him more worry by rejecting Simon.

It had been decided finally that Simon, with a new wife and an elderly father, should give up any dreams of military glory and remain at home to run the family estates and those of Jane's father, which would eventually be joined to his own estates when Jane inherited them.

For a time there was a lull. The whole country seemed to be holding its breath, waiting for hostilities to start, the first blood to be shed.

8

Belinda was in an upstairs room one morning when she heard the clatter of horses' hooves. She dashed to the window. Could it be Robert? She saw a group of half-a-dozen riders dressed in leather jerkins with broad sashes and with pistols thrust into their belts, led by a man dressed in scarlet who wore a wide-brimmed hat with a large feather. As she watched, they came to a halt before the front door and at a signal from the leader one of the men dismounted, climbed the steps, and beat loudly on the door which was opened, after a short delay, by the elderly butler.

'In the name of the King!' Belinda heard the man bellow harshly. 'We are here to speak to your master, Sir Henry Spence. Tell him we are waiting.'

Confused by this abrupt greeting, the

butler shuffled off to find Sir Henry, leaving the door open. By now the leader and three other men had also dismounted and made for the steps. Belinda realised they had come into the house without waiting to be asked when she heard the sound of their boots on the hall floor. Then came her father's hurried steps. The leader gave him no chance to speak.

'Sir Henry Spence? We are here on behalf of his royal majesty, King Charles. We take it that you are a faithful follower of the king?'

There was an undertone of menace, but Sir Henry did not need to be threatened. 'I am indeed loyal to the king. How can I help you?' he responded with dignity.

Belinda had started to make for the staircase. She was, after all, the lady of the house and should greet callers with her father, but the leader's tone made her hesitate. She quietly crept a little way down the great staircase and peered through the banisters. The leader, or possibly the officer, stood casually in the hall, showing none of the deference or respect to which Sir Henry was entitled. His men were spread out behind him, looking round as if taking note of the hall's contents.

'As you have probably heard, King Charles is calling on all gentlemen to join him, together with as many fighting men as they can muster.'

'So I have heard. However as you see, I am past fighting age and most of the men on my estate have already gone to serve their chosen leaders.'

'We have been told that. We have also been told that some of them have chosen the Parliamentary side. Can you explain why men who served you should have chosen to rebel? Did you not make the justice of the king's cause sufficiently clear to them?'

Sir Henry hesitated. 'They all knew that I support the king,' he replied, 'but there were apparently a few who held different views.'

'And you did nothing to prevent

them joining Parliament's forces?'

'How could I?' Sir Henry's voice grew stronger with rising indignation. 'They never told me their beliefs, but slipped away. I equipped those who went to serve the king. That should show my loyalty.'

'Perhaps,' was the enigmatic reply, followed by a long pause. 'However,' the officer barked suddenly, making Belinda jump, 'you can prove your loyalty in other ways. The king needs money, valuables, as well as men. Give generously, Sir Henry, and prove you are true to the king.'

These men could not be from the king, Belinda told herself. They did not look like soldiers, no written authority had been shown, and now they were demanding money, not asking for it. Silently she retraced her steps to the upper landing, and then tiptoed away from the scene below.

Sir Henry was also very disturbed.

'If you are from the king . . . ' he began, but was not allowed to say more.

'If? Are you questioning my authority?' The leader's hand was on his sword and his men were moving menacingly forward. 'Unless you and your household wish to suffer for your impertinence, you will make quite sure that you give us enough to compensate for your attitude.'

He glanced contemptuously at the servants who had ventured as far as the door from their quarters in support of their master, but who had obviously realised that they could not tackle the intruders and had not dared to advance further. Not deigning to pay them any more attention, the leader turned back to Sir Henry.

'And where is your daughter? She should be here to greet visitors.'

'My daughter is somewhere upstairs, I believe.'

'Then we shall find her there. I understand that you keep your valuables upstairs.'

'How do you know that?' Sir Henry asked sharply, but there was no reply.

Instead the group of men surrounded him and herded him towards the staircase. His protests unheard, he was gradually forced upwards to the first floor. The leader seemed to know the layout of the house for he turned towards Sir Henry's bedroom, but stopped as Belinda appeared from another room. He swept a deep bow, but Belinda faced him coldly.

'Sir, you should treat my father with more respect.'

He grinned at her, examining her slowly in a way that made her blush furiously. 'I beg your pardon, ma'am. I am afraid war means such niceties must be neglected.'

He threw open the door to a room and made for the closet which housed Sir Henry's remaining treasures. The door was locked and he turned to Sir Henry. 'Where is the key?'

Sir Henry was beyond resistance, frightened for the safety of his daughter and servants. He pointed to a desk.

The key was found, the closet opened, and Sir Henry and Belinda had to stand helplessly by as the leader went in with another man. They came out five minutes later with a half-full linen bag, but the officer was scowling with disappointment.

'You seem to have spirited away more of your treasures than was thought,' he said through clenched teeth. His eyes turned to Belinda. 'However, I am sure that your daughter is eager to make her contribution. Ma'am, where is your jewel box?'

In spite of her indignant protests her room was invaded and her jewel box emptied on the bed. The leader smiled. 'A nice collection of trinkets.'

He began to stuff them in his pockets, but Belinda darted forward and snatched one box.

'These are my mother's pearls. You are not taking those!' she dared him, hugging the box to her.

He hesitated, and then shrugged, obviously deciding against using force.

'Keep your souvenir. We'll take the rest.'

By the time they had finished ransacking the house the group had also taken the family's silver plate. Their pretence of being there on the king's behalf had been tacitly abandoned as they guessed the value of items and tried to seize choice pieces before their companions could. Finally they decided there was nothing more worth taking, and with their booty wrapped in curtains torn roughly from the windows they made their way out through the main door to where their two companions sat patiently guarding the horses. They mounted, the officer making a mocking bow of farewell. As they made off rapidly, one of the men who had stayed outside turned round and looked triumphantly at Belinda and Sir Henry and she saw his face clearly for the first time. It was John, the groom who had tried to rob Belinda on her way to France!

Her hand tightened painfully on her father's arm.

'Did you see him?' she demanded.

'Did you see John?'

Her father looked at her in bewilderment, but before she could explain the distraught housekeeper claimed her attention.

'Ma'am, Mistress Belinda — I don't know what to do!'

The servants' hall was in an uproar. A maidservant was having noisy hysterics, claiming the attention of the other female servants, some of whom seemed about to follow her example. Meanwhile Sir Henry's valet was desperately trying to find someone who would help him with the butler, who had collapsed on the floor. Belinda decided this was no time to be ladylike. She slapped the hysterical maid's face, shouted at the other women and told them not to be so foolish, and had the butler carried up to bed where he could rest and recover. Then she went to find her father. He was sitting in his study with his head in his hands and looked on the point of collapse himself.

'It's all gone!' he said despairingly.

'They have taken everything!'

'Not everything, Father,' she told him.

'You saw them!'

Belinda smiled. 'They have our silver, and most of my jewels — but you heard them say that there was not as much in the closet as they expected.'

He shook his head. 'What are you talking about?'

'Look under your mattress. Most of your gold is there. I just had time to take it to your bedroom and lock up again before they came upstairs. I am afraid I had to leave some pieces or they would have suspected.'

Sir Henry's face brightened and he hurried off to see what she had saved.

Belinda spent some minutes wondering what could be done to catch the robbers before deciding reluctantly that there was nothing. Her father could not appeal to the local magistrates for help, for those who were still in office had more urgent matters to concern them and had neither the time nor the manpower to chase thieves.

The household gradually returned to some semblance of normality, though the butler would be confined to bed for some time. Everyone was turning to Belinda for advice and instruction, and the weight of responsibility was proving a burden.

Her father was torn between regret for what he had lost and thankfulness that some had been saved, and was in an irritable mood. At one moment he even reproached her for not keeping one particular medallion. She wondered how she was supposed to have been able to choose what to save in the brief time that had been available.

She was attempting to persuade the cook that dinner must be cooked and served as normal, when she heard a shrill scream and one of the maids ran into the room.

'They're coming back!' the girl cried. 'The horsemen! They are coming up the drive!'

Belinda hurried to a window. A small

group of riders was visible, but their leader was not dressed in scarlet. He was taller, and looked somehow familiar. She stared intently, and then gasped, flew to the door and pulled it open, ran down the steps and threw herself into the arms of Robert Hetherington as he dismounted. For a moment he clasped her to him, and thankfully she rested her head on his leather jerkin. Then she straightened and pushed him away.

'Why couldn't you have come earlier?' she demanded.

'Why? What has happened?'

'We were robbed by men who pretended to be here in the king's name.'

His gaze sharpened and he turned to his followers and told them to dismount and wait for him. She saw Harry, who smiled and waved to her as Robert gently led Belinda indoors and persuaded her to give him a clear account of what had happened. She had just finished when her father hurried up and added his colourful account of his sufferings and emotions, to which Robert listened patiently.

'I am afraid you are not the only victims,' he said soberly. 'We have been hearing reports of this gang who pretend to be from the king and then seize anything of value they can find. How long is it since they left?'

'Less than three hours.'

Robert's smile was not pleasant and his golden eyes glittered.

'They may not have gone far. I only decided to come here this morning so they will not be expecting us to be in the area.' His hand rested on his pistol. 'We will follow them.'

'Do you think you may get my gold back?' Sir Henry asked hopefully.

'Perhaps. Anyway, it is important that we deal with this gang. Too many people believe that they are here on the king's behalf, and that is turning their victims against his majesty.'

He strode towards the door. Belinda hurried after him. 'Robert!'

He stopped and turned. Gazing at him, she saw that he looked dusty and tired with travelling. She drew close to him and placed her hand on his arm.

'Can you not rest for a little? We can feed you and your men.'

He put his hand over hers. She was conscious of the warmth of his touch.

'Thank you, but the sooner we pick up their trail, the more likely we are to catch the thieves.'

'Take care. They frightened me,' she murmured.

'Worry not. I myself have been known to frighten villains.' He smiled wryly. 'This was supposed to be a courtesy call, a chance to see you and have a brief rest from the cares of war.' He took her hands, lifted them and kissed them. 'Well, now I must leave you again.'

Then he and his men were gone.

The day dragged slowly by. Belinda stayed up long after the rest of the household had gone to bed, but no messenger came to the door with good or bad news. It was nearing noon the following morning when one lone horseman rode up to the house. Summoned by a maid, Belinda found Harry waiting in the hall, holding a saddlebag. He bowed and held the bag out to her with his left hand.

'I think you will find most of your father's coins here, Mistress Belinda, and some trinkets which are probably yours, but I regret we could not find the silver. It was probably too heavy to carry so the thieves will have hidden it somewhere.'

She took the bag but let it drop to the floor, looking at him closely.

'What is the matter with your right arm? Are you hurt?'

His familiar smile appeared. 'One of the thieves tried to break it with a cudgel, but it is bruised, not broken, fortunately.'

'So you found them! I'm sorry, that makes me sound like a fool because obviously you did.'

He nodded. 'Yes, we caught the rats

— and this time they won't get away because we have handed them over to the king's officers.'

'And you are all well?'

The smile glimmered again. 'A few little cuts and bruises like mine, but Master Hetherington is safe and well.'

She blushed. He had known she was really only interested in one person. Now she looked beyond him eagerly.

'When will Master Hetherington be here so we can thank him?'

He shook his head. 'Master Hetherington is not coming back. That is why he sent me to return your property. A rider from the King found him yesterday with a message ordering him to go north without delay.'

'North? Where? Why must he go north?'

There was no smile now. 'The king has set up his standard at Nottingham and bade all his friends join him. Essex and the forces of Parliament are marching north from London. The real war has begun, Mistress Belinda.'

Belinda knew there was nothing she could do. Robert had turned aside from his mission to help her, and now he had to follow the king, even though he doubted that king's wisdom and actions.

She forced a smile. 'Is there anything you need that we can provide?'

'Thank you, but I think we have everything we need. Do not be too eager to give your stores away, Mistress Belinda. There are hard times coming.'

She saw him to his horse and he gathered up his reins and prepared to ride off. Then suddenly he turned back to her.

'Forgive me. I almost forgot. Master Hetherington asked me to give his good wishes to you and Master Simon for a long and happy life together.'

'But Simon and I are not . . . ' Belinda began, but it was too late. Harry had kicked his horse into action and was already galloping away.

She went to tell her father the good news. He was delighted, and was soon examining his rescued treasures for signs of damage.

'Gold is a soft metal, you know,' he told his daughter. 'It marks easily.'

He did not ask what had happened to the men who had saved his gold.

★　★　★

Life went on, though difficulties were increasing. Sir Henry and his friends in their rural setting were strong Royalists, but found themselves becoming isolated from the surrounding areas because London and much of the eastern counties supported Parliament. Many of the small comforts of life were no longer obtainable and the usual round of visits and social meetings had been virtually abandoned. Belinda found herself growing lonely. Her father had retreated from the problems of daily life, spending almost all his time in his library studying his rescued hoard.

They usually dined in almost total

silence, but one evening Sir Henry was obviously in an irritable mood. He criticised the food, complained about the service and told Belinda that she was letting the servants do as they liked. This was too much. She looked at him challengingly and spoke like an equal rather than a dutiful daughter.

'What is really upsetting you, Father?'

'Nothing — it is what I have pointed out.'

'You know the difficulties I have to deal with. There must be some other cause for your ill temper.'

He scowled, threw down his napkin and seemed about to push back his chair and leave. Then the anger seemed to desert him. He gave a great sigh.

'I am sorry. I am tired of this life we are forced to lead nowadays. I cannot pursue my studies because I am unable to visit my friends in London and letters to scholars are not answered. In short, I am frustrated and bored, but I know there is no escape.'

Belinda looked at her plate and

fidgeted with a knife, and then looked up at him. 'There is something we could do, Father. I have been thinking about it for some time, but I am not sure you would agree to it.'

'Tell me what you are thinking of and let me decide.'

'Well,' she began hesitantly, 'as you have said, there is little for us here now. Perhaps, sometime in the future, life may return to what it was, but that may not be for years. Instead of waiting, we could go to your sister in France.' Sir Henry was about to speak but she held up her hand. 'Please, let me finish, Father. We would not be the first. I have heard that many gentlefolk are sending their families across the Channel to keep them out of harm's way. Your sister said she would welcome me back at any time, and I am sure she would be equally glad to see you. You and her husband have much in common. He is also an art lover and collector and he admired the treasures you sent to France.'

Sir Henry shook his head. 'I will not live on my sister's charity!'

'You would not be penniless! Her husband is already guarding a treasure which belongs to you and we could take what is left here. Admittedly, you may have to sell a few minor items, but you would still be wealthy.'

Sir Henry still looked uncertain so she went on persuasively. 'The Count would be delighted to help with your studies. He could introduce you to many learned men in Paris.'

'But what about this house and my estates?'

'Walter Jones is an efficient steward.'

In fact she was aware that the steward was already running the estates with very little help from Sir Henry.

'I will think about it,' was her father's final statement that night.

But in the morning he sought her out.

'I have decided we should go to France,' he announced, as though the idea had been his own. 'There are a few matters to attend to, of course, but we should be able to leave within a week.

'Yes, Father,' Belinda said submissively, inwardly triumphant. In France she would be freed from the responsibility of housekeeping and making decisions her father should have taken care of. And she would leave behind both Simon and Robert Hetherington. She could make a fresh start.

9

Arrangements were quickly made. While Belinda and Sir Henry were away, a couple of servants would sleep in the house and see that no harm came to it. The horses were sent into the care of neighbours, and Walter Jones received with ill-concealed pleasure the news that he would be in sole charge of the estates for an unknown length of time. Belinda and her father took their leave of their friends and acquaintances and left for Dover. This time they travelled in their coach with Sir Henry's valet and the maid who had replaced Sarah. Escorted by Simon and two of his servants, they reached the coast and put up at an inn in Dover while Simon and his men took the coach back.

So far, so good, but their troubles started when they looked for a ship to take them across the Channel. With both sides in the war patrolling the seas, there were far fewer craft willing to make the trip. As Belinda had told her father, many people had decided that France was safer than England, so the few places available on ships were hotly sought after and very expensive. Sir Henry spent a couple of days combing the docks without luck, and it was Belinda, trailing along with him, who saw a familiar figure preparing to board a fishing boat.

'Good evening, captain,' she called out. 'When do you leave on your next trip? I'm sure you will have room for us on board.'

'This is a fishing boat. We don't take passengers,' the man said curtly, not even bothering to look at her.

'Perhaps not on every trip, but I have enjoyed your hospitality previously,' she persevered.

Now he did turn and look at her, and his face cracked in a wide grin.

'I remember! There were you three youngsters and the man who had been to the Americas. Did all go well?'

'Very well, thank you, but now my father and I and our two servants need passage to France.'

He shook his head. 'It's more dangerous, mistress, I must warn you.'

'We are ready to take the risk.'

'The price is higher.'

'We can pay.'

Space on The Pelican did indeed cost Sir Henry a surprising amount, but it got them a safe crossing to France, where a hired carriage took them through Normandy to Count Beaumetz's grey castle. There Belinda was instantly recognised and she and her companions were welcomed in.

'Are the Count and the Countess still here?' she enquired, afraid that if the couple had returned to Paris it would complicate matters. But she was assured that they were still in Normandy and that they were even then being informed of her arrival.

Seconds later rapid footsteps could be heard. The footman hastily opened the door as Aunt Maria almost ran in and flung her arms around Belinda. 'I am so happy to see you! But what has happened? Has my brother sent you?'

Belinda hugged her aunt.

'He hasn't sent me, Aunt Maria. He has brought me. Look!'

Sir Henry held out his arms to his sister and there was a joyful reunion. The Count appeared, greeting his brother-in-law with warmth and respect.

'I have often admired the pieces you entrusted to me, but I lack your knowledge of their history and the artists. Now I look forward to hearing all about them.'

He could not have said anything better. Sir Henry swelled with pride and decided that living in another man's house might not be too much of an ordeal.

Count Beaumetz led Sir Henry away to his study and Aunt Maria hurried Belinda off to her private rooms. The servants were already being cared for by their French counterparts.

'You look tired, my dear,' Aunt Maria commented when they were comfortably settled.

'That is due to the journey — and to life in England recently.'

Her aunt nodded sympathetically. 'We have heard stories. Still, we will look after you well here. Do I understand that you and my brother have come to stay for some time?'

'If you will have us.'

'Of course!' Her aunt stood up and twirled round. 'Now, look at me. Do you notice anything?'

Belinda looked closely, but Aunt Maria was draped in full, flowing garments and it was difficult to tell what she was supposed to observe.

'A new gown?' Belinda ventured, but her aunt shook her head, laughing.

'Not my clothes! Something much more important!'

Belinda looked again, closely; and then gasped.

'Aunt Maria! You are . . . '

'I am with child! I am to have a baby

in about three months' time.'

'Sit down,' Belinda urged her hastily. 'Then tell me all about it.'

Her aunt obeyed, eyes shining.

'Soon after you left I began to feel ill each morning, and I was very tired. I was afraid that I had caught some disease, so I sent for the doctor. He examined me, asked me some questions, and then laughed and told me that I wasn't ill, I was having a baby. After all these years! But apparently it sometimes happens that a childless woman conceives as she grows older, and that is what has happened to me.'

'What did your husband say when he learned this wonderful news?'

'After such a long time, he found it difficult to believe at first. Now he is delighted and I am cherished like the most precious thing on earth.'

'And is all well?'

'Very well. I merely sleep a lot.' She laughed happily, and then looked at Belinda with sudden concern. 'Of course, this means that we are staying in Normandy at least until the child is born. If you were hoping I would take you to Paris, I am afraid I must disappoint you.'

Belinda shook her head.

'Do not concern yourself with that. I shall be quite happy here with you.'

Her aunt looked relieved.

'Perhaps Simon will be happier if you stay here away from the temptations of Paris. How is he?'

'Married, to Jane,' Belinda stated baldly and went on to explain what had happened.

'Good!' her aunt said comfortably when she had finished. 'He was very dull. You would not have been happy with him.'

The household quickly absorbed its new members. The Count and Sir Henry were delighted to find that they could discuss their individual hobbies with each other and both praised the other's understanding and knowledge. Belinda could relax and enjoy the comfort of the well-run and happy establishment. Instead of being lonely and bored, Aunt Maria was now the centre of her little world, carefully cherished by all around her. Belinda felt that this happy period was removed from real life and that the problems they had left behind would inevitably catch up with them, but meanwhile she walked and sat with her aunt, took gentle exercise in the gardens, and listened politely when her father praised some item of the count's collection. Inevitably there were times when she fretted at the lack of purposeful activity, and regretted Paris. At this rate she would be twenty and past marriageable age before she met any eligible young men!

'What happened to the guests who were here with me before — Madame St Claud and Monsieur Brissac?' she asked one day.

Her aunt sat up and leant forward, eager to impart gossip.

'Monsieur Brissac has not been seen since he left here,' she told Belinda. 'It is believed that he must have left the country to avoid his creditors. As for Madame St Claud, she shocked everybody when she married a merchant — little more than a shopkeeper! He is wealthy enough, but of course she can no longer be received in polite society.'

One morning Belinda and her maid set off for a nearby village to enjoy the weekly market. They returned happy, having bought themselves a few small treats. As they made their way back through the castle courtyard a manservant turned and doffed his hat. Belinda acknowledged this courtesy with a nod of her head, then looked again as the man stood looking at her with an expectant air. Recognising him, she almost dropped her purchases.

'Harry! it is you!'

He smiled at her like an old friend.

'Miss Belinda! My master will be pleased to see you.'

'Robert — Master Hetherington is here?'

'We have only just arrived. I believe

the Count is receiving him now.'

Belinda thrust her parcels into the arms of her maid, gathered up her skirts, and ran into the house to the reception room. She stopped abruptly as she reached the door, straightened her gown and patted her hair, and then knocked at the door and went in. The Count and Robert were seated together, drinking a glass of wine. As Belinda came in Robert looked up and his golden eyes widened. He put his glass down and stood up hastily.

'Belinda — Mistress Spence!'

She came forward, holding out her hands. 'It is so good to see you again!' she said.

For a moment they gazed at each other, and then he took her right hand and kissed it formally.

'It is a pleasure — and a surprise — to meet again here, Mistress Belinda. Are you with your friends?'

'I am here with my father. Now he will be able to thank you for rescuing our goods from those thieves.'

'It was my duty to preserve the good name of my king.'

His behaviour was formal, his manner almost cold. Belinda decided he felt constrained by the presence of the Count and excused herself, saying she wished to show her aunt her purchases.

Belinda saw Robert next at dinner, which did not afford a suitable opportunity for an intimate conversation. She learned that he was there once again as an emissary from his brother, contacting friends of the English king, and had already spent some time in Paris.

'But Paris is full of Parliament's spies,' he told his little audience. 'Many at the French court are not sure whether the Royalists or the Parliamentarians will win in the end, and are unwilling to commit themselves — at least in public.' He turned to the count. 'That is why I am so grateful to you, sir, for allowing me to stay here for a while. I can contact many people with more freedom here, and receive the occasional visitor.'

'How long will you be here?' Belinda asked.

'A few weeks,' he said, addressing her directly for the first time.

She relaxed. There would be time to talk.

10

To Belinda's pleasure, Robert Hetherington sought her out the very next day. 'The Count has told me that you are no longer betrothed to Simon Gregory,' were his opening words after a brief greeting.

'More than that. Simon and Jane were married to each other before my father and I left England.'

He leaned back against his seat, frowning deeply. 'So Master Gregory broke his promise to you so that he could marry that timid, tearful girl?'

'No!' Belinda almost snarled. 'I broke off the betrothal when I realised they had fallen in love — and that I did not want to marry him anyway!'

'Then you did the right thing. He would have bored you, and your quick temper would have upset him.'

She glared at him, but he said no

more and soon he excused himself. She reflected as she watched him walk away that now he knew the true situation, he would soon come looking for her again.

But somehow that time never came. Robert was away most of the time calling on various French gentlemen, and when he was at the castle he always seemed too busy. His behaviour to her in public remained formal, almost unfriendly, and finally Belinda decided that he was deliberately avoiding her. She was hurt. Hadn't they become close during their adventures? Reluctantly, she decided that perhaps he regarded her as just a silly girl whom he had been compelled to help, but whose company he now found boring. Maybe he had seen those kisses, which she remembered so vividly, as a small reward for his efforts on her behalf. Well, she would not pester him. In her turn, she avoided him whenever she could. At dinner, occasionally she was aware that he was looking at her, but

183

she carefully avoided catching his eye.

Then came a crisis which took everyone by surprise. Robert had been away for some days on one of his mysterious errands and Sir Henry and the count had ridden out to visit a neighbour with an interesting collection of cameos, Aunt Maria had decided to spend a lazy day in bed, and Belinda was working on some embroidery. Suddenly Belinda became aware of a disturbance nearby. There were cries, and the sound of running feet. She stood up just as her maid burst into the room.

'Mistress, come quickly!' she cried, wide-eyed. 'The Countess has gone into labour, and nobody knows what to do!'

Belinda hurried to her aunt's room, her maid close behind. A cluster of maidservants by the door parted to let her in.

'Aunt Maria!' she cried. Her aunt lay back on her pillows, eyes shut, pain distorting her face.

The Countess opened her eyes and

tears rolled down her cheeks. 'It should not happen for weeks yet,' she whispered. 'Something must have gone awry.'

'Have the doctor and midwife been sent for?' Belinda demanded.

Her aunt shook her head. 'I know not.'

As Belinda turned towards the door, her aunt panicked. 'Stay with me!'

'I will be back soon, Aunt, I promise you.'

She left the room, closed the door and looked at the maids.

'You!' she said, pointing to her aunt's maid. 'Go to the servant's hall and send one of the grooms for the doctor as quickly as possible.' She turned to another. 'Do you know where the midwife lives?' The girl nodded. 'Send another groom there. He must not come back without her.'

As the two women hurried away she turned to the remainder. 'As for the rest of you, make sure that there is plenty of hot water and clean linen.'

As the maids scattered, she saw with mixed surprise and relief that Robert was hurrying towards her.

'I have just returned but I have already heard the news,' he said briefly. 'Is there anything I can do?'

She grimaced. 'That depends. Do you know anything about childbirth?'

'No, though I have helped cows deliver their calves often enough.'

She laughed involuntarily. 'We may need your skills if the doctor doesn't hurry. Please find the count and my uncle, tell them what is happening and bring them back as quickly as you can. Now I must go to my aunt.'

There was little she could do except murmur comforting words while her aunt held her hand so tightly that she felt it was being bruised. Fortunately it was not long before the doctor arrived, and then the midwife, so she was able to leave Aunt Maria in their care. Then the Count returned, frantic with worry, and she was able to assure him that everything possible was being done for his wife. After that there was nothing to do but wait.

★ ★ ★

Over an hour later, the doctor came down the small morning room where Belinda and the Count and Sir Henry were waiting. Belinda tensed, then saw that the doctor was smiling, and she felt weak with relief. He spoke directly to the Count.

'Congratulations! You have a son, and both he and your wife are well.'

The Count gave a harsh sigh. 'But the child is weeks early!'

The doctor shook his head. 'I told your wife that we could not be certain when the child would come. He is maybe a week or two early, but no more. He is a fine boy.'

'Can I see them?'

The doctor stretched out his hand. 'Come with me, my lord.'

The celebrations that followed were mixed with relief. Belinda viewed the

187

small, red-faced scrap in a shawl and swore he was the most beautiful child she had ever seen. Her aunt received her congratulations, and then fell into a deep sleep.

Belinda went out into the garden and sank down on a bench, glad of the peace and quiet. Robert Hetherington found her there.

'I understand that all is well,' he commented, sitting down beside her.

'Yes. They are so happy! The christening will be a splendid occasion.'

'I am afraid I will be gone by then,' he said heavily. 'I have received a letter. The King wishes me to go to Virginia to raise funds from his followers there. But my brother knows that my heart is not in this conflict between King and Parliament. He has discussed the situation with me and has decided to give me his estates in Virginia in exchange for my property in England. I shall sail from Southampton to America in the near future to carry out the King's wishes, but I do not expect ever to return.'

Belinda was suddenly full of cold, aching despair.

'Then I shall never see you again!'

He ran his fingers through his short black hair, frowning. When he finally spoke, his words shocked her.

'Come to Virginia with me — as my wife.'

She stared at him blankly. 'You have avoided me, virtually ignored me, since you came here, and now you ask me to marry you. Are you mad?'

She faced him angrily and he looked at her with exasperation.

'I had no choice! Since I came to France I have spent my time dealing with opponents who wanted me dead. How could I approach you, even in friendship, when I was never sure I would survive the day? And there was always the possibility that if they realised that you were anything more than an acquaintance, you would have been in danger as well. They might have taken you hostage and used you as a tool against me. It is a tactic they have used with others.'

Her hand rose to her throat. 'They want to kill you?'

He smiled with grim satisfaction.

'This week the problem has been solved. They will never threaten anybody again. Now, answer me. Will you marry me?'

He grasped her hands and she closed her eyes.

'We hardly know each other,' she said uncertainly, making a last attempt to be sensible.

'We know each other well enough. But above all, when I look at you I know you are the woman for me.' He released her hands and drew away from her slightly. 'I have been too sudden. Think things over and give me your answer when you can.'

Suddenly the way ahead seemed simple. Why had she not realised that she had loved Robert Hetherington ever since that first journey to France?

'There is no need,' she laughed, abandoning common sense. 'I will marry you, Robert.'

His face lit up, but he shook his head warningly.

'I am asking a lot of you. If you marry me, you will never see your country or your friends again. And will your father not only give his consent, but agree to come with us? I do not wish to separate you from him for ever.'

He went on, 'Virginia can offer you much, but I will not always be content with the estates I have been given. My desire is to explore, to learn what else there is in that new land. There may well be danger, and you would have to be ready to take on more responsibility than in England. Virginia would be a challenge for us both.'

Belinda considered briefly what he had said. But she had already left her country. Her friends might wonder about her occasionally, but they had their own lives to live. She smiled, her eyes shining.

'You are offering me what I wish for — a change from the old, ordered life which I sometimes felt was stifling me. I am not afraid of challenges. And I want to be with you.'

'What about your father?'

'I think he could be persuaded to come. Virginia would offer him the way of life to which he was accustomed in England before the troubles began. And if we point out that he will be much nearer the source of all those golden treasures from South America, he will beg to come with us!'

Now Robert kissed her long and lovingly.

'I thought you were beautiful when I first met you, and I have learned that you are brave and intelligent,' he said at last. 'I love you truly, and I believe we will make a good pair.' He stood up and held out his hand. 'Let us go and inform your father that today he has not only gained a nephew, but also a son-in-law.'

Hand in hand they went together to face the future.

We do hope that you have enjoyed reading this large print book.

Did you know that all of our titles are available for purchase?

We publish a wide range of high quality large print books including:
Romances, Mysteries, Classics
General Fiction
Non Fiction and Westerns

Special interest titles available in large print are:
The Little Oxford Dictionary
Music Book, Song Book
Hymn Book, Service Book

Also available from us courtesy of Oxford University Press:
Young Readers' Dictionary
(large print edition)
Young Readers' Thesaurus
(large print edition)

For further information or a free brochure, please contact us at:
Ulverscroft Large Print Books Ltd.,
The Green, Bradgate Road, Anstey,
Leicester, LE7 7FU, England.
Tel: (00 44) **0116 236 4325**
Fax: (00 44) **0116 234 0205**

Other titles in the
Linford Romance Library:

WAITING FOR A
STAR TO FALL

Wendy Kremer

Lucy and Ethan grew up together.
Lucy worshipped Ethan from afar
and was disenchanted when he left
for university, and didn't return. She
hadn't realised that this was because
of his family's hidden problems.
Lucy is now the village librarian and
Ethan is a well-known author. When
Ethan comes back to the village and
into her life again, can he shed his
obsession with the past? Will they
master the obstacles and find each
other before it's too late?